CAPTURED!

Nate gestured for his family to stop, and drew rein. "Hold it while I see what's going on," he said quietly. He slid off his horse and crept to the opening. Dense vegetation cloaked a narrow trail and prevented him from seeing what lay beyond. Cautiously, he stepped into the open, and as he leveled his rifle he remembered to his dismay that he had forgotten to reload it. He had broken his first law of survival.

Above him, leaves shook. Nate looked up and saw two husky warriors balanced on a stout limb.

They had just dropped a net.

WILDERNESS

#23:

THE LOST VALLEY

DAVID THOMPSON

LEISURE BOOKS   NEW YORK CITY

Dedicated to Judy, Joshua, and Shane.

A LEISURE BOOK®

January 1998

Published by

Dorchester Publishing Co., Inc.
276 Fifth Avenue
New York, NY 10001

ISBN 0-8439-4346-7

THE LOST VALLEY

Chapter One

The Rocky Mountains were magnificent in the summer. Emerald hills blended into stark ranges capped by pristine snow. Cottonwoods and willows wound along rivers and streams. Firs, spruce, and aspens adorned the higher regions. The land was green, ripe, lush.

Wildlife thrived. White-tailed deer foraged in the lowlands, while their black-tailed cousins roamed the upper slopes. Elk claimed the high meadows but had to share their domain with small herds of shaggy mountain buffalo. Bears were much in evidence. Smaller creatures—chipmunks, squirrels, rabbits, and the like—were everywhere.

Nate King had lived in the mountains for sixteen years, yet he never tired of Nature's wondrous spectacle. Every day brought something new. Each moment was different from all those that went before it.

Nate never missed the dull sameness of city life, the boring routine, the daily grind that broke a person's spirit

7

and made him feel as if he were no more than cogs in a machine. City dwellers were like cattle cooped up in small pens, with nothing to do and nowhere to go. Day in and day out they suffered in a prison of their own making.

Not Nate. Give him the raw wilderness any day. Give him true freedom: being able to do whatever he wanted, whenever he wanted. Give him a life where he was not beholden to anyone for anything, where he need not account to any man for his actions.

These were the thoughts that occupied the mountaineer as he wound up a game trail to a sawtooth ridge and reined up.

He had no idea of the picture he presented. It had been a coon's age since Nate had last seen his reflection in a mirror. If he had bothered to look, he would have seen a tall, broad-shouldered man with piercing blue eyes, raven-black hair, and a cropped beard. A buckskin hunting shirt and leggings covered his powerful frame; moccasins protected his feet. Slanted across his chest were a powder horn and ammo pouch. A possibles bag hung under his left arm. In a beaded sheath on his right hip nestled a Green River knife; on his left hip was a tomahawk. Wedged under his wide leather belt were two flintlocks; cradled in his elbow, a heavy Hawken.

Behind Nate rode his wife, Winona. A full-blooded Shoshone, she wore a fringed dress she had made herself, just as she had crafted her husband's clothes. Her luxurious dark hair hung in neat braids. A necklace of blue beads lent a splash of color. She was lovely by any standard, but she was not one of those women who took on airs over her own beauty. As Nate had once put it, she was as levelheaded as the day was long.

In Winona's wake rode a miniature version of herself. Evelyn, their seven-and-a-half-year-old daughter, was a bundle of energy. She always had a sparkle to her eyes, a bounce to her step. She was their pride and joy.

That did not mean they loved the last rider any less. Zachary King, their son, held his head high as he rode up over the crest. The confidence of youth was in his gaze. An air of invincibility wreathed him like a crown. He was a few months shy of sixteen, full of life, cocky and adventurous. Experience had not yet taught him humility. Hardship had not yet bred wisdom. Now, bringing his bay to a halt, he asked, "Why'd you stop, Pa? I thought you wanted to reach those twin peaks yonder by sundown."

Nate King did not answer right away. The peaks to which his son referred were a good twenty miles to the southwest. Of more immediate interest to him were wispy gray tendrils wafting skyward less than a mile from the ridge. Nodding at them, he responded, "When are you going to learn to always keep your eyes skinned, son? First things first."

Zach flushed with embarrassment. No warrior worthy of the name would miss spotting that smoke. And above all else, more than anything he had ever yearned for, Zach desired to be a full-fledged Shoshone warrior.

The youth had always been partial to his mother's people. Part of each year was spent living with them. Most accepted him for what he was, unlike many whites who tended to look down their noses at 'breeds.

One day soon, Zach planned to take up with the Shoshones permanently. To have a fine lodge of his own, to be accorded a position of honor at tribal councils, these were his goals, his dream.

At the moment, though, Zach mentally kicked himself and said, "Utes, you reckon?"

Nate King would not hazard a guess. It might be, but he had made a point of fighting shy of Ute country. For more years than he cared to recollect, the Utes had tried their darnedest to oust him from the remote valley his family called home. Recently, a fragile truce had been put into effect. But Nate knew there were plenty of warriors who would like nothing better than to count coup at his expense.

Winona regarded the smoke anxiously. Should they run into anyone unfriendly, it would be partly her fault. After all, she was the one who had insisted the family needed to get away from their cabin after being cooped up most of the winter. She was the one who suggested they venture into new territory, that they go somewhere they had never been before.

Here they were, eleven days out. So far as she knew, no white man had ever set foot there. Nor any Shoshones, for that matter.

"We should avoid them, husband," Winona said in her flawless English. It was a great source of pride to her that she spoke the white man's tongue so well. She had a knack, as Nate would say. "They might be hostile."

"I agree." Nate had no hankering to court trouble. The mountains teemed with savage beasts and even more brutal men, two-legged rabid wolves who would slaughter his loved ones without a moment's hesitation.

Little Evelyn rose on her pony for a better look-see. "What if they're nice folks, Ma?" she asked.

Winona looked at her offspring and smiled. *My sweet, darling Blue Flower*, she thought, using her daughter's Shoshone name. *So young. So innocent.* "We cannot take the chance."

"But how do we ever get to meet new people if we don't take chances?" Evelyn asked.

Nate shifted in the saddle. It was the kind of question only a child would ask, only someone who believed the world was made of sugar and spice and everything nice. "There's a time and a place for meeting new folks. This isn't it."

"Why not?"

10

The Lost Valley

Logic was no match for innocence, Nate decided. Rather than go into a long-winded spiel about the nature of the human race, he resorted to the one argument every parent could count on. "Because I say so."

"Shucks. That's no reason, Pa."

No, it wasn't, but Nate was not about to admit as much. Reining westward, he started down a steep slope bordered on the right by talus and on the left by a tangled deadfall. "Be mighty careful," he warned.

Accidents were a constant dread. It wouldn't take much. A single misstep, a careless slip, and one of them could well be crippled for life—or worse. It was the one drawback to wilderness living, Nate mused. There were no doctors just around the corner, no convenient hospitals nearby.

The mountain man was consoled somewhat by the fact that accidents were part and parcel of life everywhere, not just in the mountains. How well he remembered that time back in New York City when he had almost been run down by a wagon. And that incident when he had fallen off a pier and nearly been crushed by a passing boat.

Why the Almighty had seen fit to set up things so that accidents could happen, Nate had no idea. There was a lot about life he did not understand, and probably never would. Sometimes it seemed as if the more he learned, the more mysteries cropped up.

Zach King was the last to descend. He happened to glance one last time toward the smoke, and was startled to spot shadowy figures flit through trees west of it. "Pa!" he said, speaking softly even though the distance to the trees was too great for anyone to overhear. When his father turned, Zach pointed.

Nate caught sight of five or six vague shapes as they vanished into the vegetation. He could not distinguish details, but his impression was that they were Indians. "We need to hunt cover," he cautioned.

A stand of pines offered a haven. Dismounting, Nate moved to a vantage point overlooking the narrow valley. The smoke issued from dense growth that flanked a stream. Hills rimmed the valley to the west, and they, in turn, were dwarfed by a snow-crowned range. It was toward a gap in those hills that the figures had been heading.

Zach slid up close to his father. Eager to be of help, he said, "Anything?" And when Nate shook his head, Zach stepped to a tree, leaned his rifle against the trunk, then leaped straight up. As agile as a monkey, he seized a limb, whipped his lean body upward, and climbed.

Nate did not object. His son had the right notion. From high up, Zach would be able to see better.

Winona admired her son's dexterity. Stalking Coyote, as the Shoshones called him, was one of the best riders, swimmers, and climbers of all the boys in the tribe. His prowess was so exceptional that great feats were expected of him in the years to come. A mighty warrior of promise, her uncle rated him.

Evelyn toyed with the idea of climbing the tree, too. She did not see why her brother should have all the fun. But then again, it was a serious situation, and her parents might not take kindly to her acting the fool. So she stayed put.

Zach was careful to climb on the side of the bole opposite the camp. After going as high as he dared, he scanned the heavily forested terrain. There was no sign of the strangers. He could see the campfire, though, and what appeared to be a man lying next to it. He reported as much to his father.

"Awful peculiar" was Nate's assessment. Indians did not make a habit of sleeping in the middle of the day. "Any horses?"

"Not unless they're real well hid."

"All right. Come on down."

Nate faced a dilemma. It would be foolhardy to cross the valley. But going around would delay them a full day, maybe more. Nor did laying low appeal to him. There was no telling when the makers of that fire would douse it and move on. Maybe that very afternoon, maybe in a few days, maybe longer. "I'm going down there," he announced.

"Count me in, Pa," Zach said.

"And Evelyn and I," Winona threw in. "We will not be left behind," she added when her husband opened his mouth as if to object. "Remember. You made the rule that we should never be separated."

"I meant for more than short spells," Nate hedged. Truth was, he had laid down the rule to ensure that none of them, but especially the children, fell prey to any of the thousand and one perils travelers might confront.

"We are all going."

Nate hid a frown by pretending to be interested in the smoke. Winona had used *that* tone, the one she always did when she put her foot down. It would take forever to persuade her to change her mind, barring a miracle. "Let me check by my lonesome," he proposed. "If the coast is clear, I'll signal."

"Who will cover your backside?" asked Zach, who had clambered to the lowest limb. Looping his legs around it, he dangled upside down, winked at his sister, then executed an acrobatic flip that resulted in a perfect upright landing. Reclaiming his rifle, he took his place at his father's elbow.

Sometimes, Nate reflected, being a husband and a father was a lot like being a tree. A man had to learn when to bend with the wind. "We'll walk the horses. Evelyn, stick to your mother like her shadow."

"Too bad we don't have blackberries handy, huh, Pa?"

"Blackberries?"

"Then I could smear myself with the juice and be just like a real shadow."

Where kids came up with comments like that, Nate would never know. His stallion's reins in hand, he led the way to the base of the ridge, sticking to dense timber wherever possible. The valley floor was more open. Scattered boulders, random clusters of trees, and tall brush provided some cover.

Nate's nerves were on edge. When a chipmunk burst out of nowhere and commenced chattering in fury at having its domain invaded, he spun and thumbed back the Hawken's hammer. Another fraction of an instant, and he'd have blown it to bits. Calming himself, he advanced, his rifle level.

Zach King tingled with excitement also, but for a reason completely different from his father's. All he could think about was the likelihood of counting coup. Every Shoshone boy shared his ambition. Proving their courage in war was the key to one day being a great leader like Pah-da-hewak-um-da or his brother Moh-woom-hah.

Winona and Evelyn brought up the rear, leading their horses. Like her husband, Winona was armed with a Hawken and a brace of pistols. Thanks to his patient tutelage, she could shoot as well as most free trappers, a rarity among Indian women. He had insisted she learn, for her own sake as well as that of their children.

Several hundred yards from the campsite, in a copse of deciduous trees, Nate raised an arm to signal a halt At a gesture from him, the rest tied their horses to low limbs or saplings. Nate crept to the edge of the next open space. The smoke had turned almost black, and an odd sickly sweet scent filled the air—a scent he felt certain he should recognize.

The Lost Valley

"Want me to scout it out?" Zach asked hopefully. As a scout he would make first contact, possibly draw first blood.

"You're to cover me, remember?" Nate said testily. His son's thirst for glory had not escaped his notice, and he could not say in all honestly that he entirely approved. Oh, he realized why Zach was so het up to prove himself. As an adopted Shoshone, Nate had likewise adopted some of their customs. But counting coup was not one he subscribed to. Bloodshed, in his estimation, was never worthy of praise. He had seen too much of it to ever glorify it.

"Not a peep out of anyone," Nate advised as he cat-footed forward. The sweet smell grew stronger, reminding him, strangely enough, of the first buffalo surround he had been on, of the cloying odor that rose from the scores of butchered animals afterward. A disturbing premonition came over him, and his gut formed into a knot.

Among a bunch of willows, Nate motioned for his family to hunker. "Stay here. I'll holler if it's safe."

"But, Pa—" Zach began.

Nate's glare silenced him. Silently, the big mountain man glided closer. He was an arrow's flight from the flickering flames when he heard a low, wavering groan. Someone was in immense agony. A little farther, a horse nickered, a feeble whinny, barely audible. Threading through cottonwoods, Nate came to the clearing where the camp had been set up. An overturned rack of dried elk meat explained why the Indians had been there.

His initial impression was that someone had traipsed around the clearing painting patches of grass and some of the surrounding growth with bright red paint. But of course, it wasn't paint.

It was blood.

15

Chapter Two

A more ghastly spectacle was hard to imagine. It was one of the most horrible scenes of rampant bloodletting Nate King had ever witnessed, rank butchery of the worst order. Stunned by the sheer magnitude of the slaughter, he surveyed the carnage, piecing together what had happened.

The victims were Utes. A hunting party of ten had been in the valley a couple of days, judging by the number of strips on the giant spilled meat rack. They had slain several elk, carved the carcasses up, and hung the meat to dry.

The attack must have come swiftly, taking them completely by surprise. Nate based his conclusion on the fact that most had fallen without a weapon in hand. A bow lay next to one man, a war club was clutched in the stiff fingers of a second, while a third warrior had gone down swinging a knife. The rest were sprawled in gory displays of violent death, their hands empty even though knives

16

rested in sheaths on their hips or bows and quivers were slung over their backs.

Since the fire had not yet gone out, Nate reckoned that the attack had taken place sometime during the early-morning hours, perhaps at daybreak. Maybe only a few of the Utes had been up, the rest struck down as they leaped to their feet.

But struck down by whom? That was the question. Nate warily emerged from concealment, pivoting to the right and the left, ready to blast anything that moved. His scalp prickled as he stared close up at the grisly handi-work of their attacker. He realized that he had it all wrong. It wasn't so much *who* as it was *what*.

Nothing human could have inflicted the wounds Nate saw on the nearest warrior. His chest had been ripped wide open, the flesh peeled back like the skin of an orange, the ribs exposed. Half the bones were shattered, the white spikes jutting obscenely. His left arm had been severed at the shoulder and was nowhere in the vicinity.

As Nate edged closer, he saw that the warrior's innards had been partially devoured. It churned his stomach. Fighting the queasiness, he bent down. On the warrior's thigh were four scarlet furrows. Claw marks they were, but unlike any Nate was familiar with. And he knew every animal that inhabited the wild.

Cats, wolves, bears, they all had five claws. Granted, sometimes the smallest claw would not show. But bear claws left wide gashes, and these were slender. Wolf claws dug shallow, but these were deep. Painter claws were thin and they dug deep, rending flesh neatly, as knives would. In this instance, the claws had ripped ragged grooves.

Bewildered, Nate went on. His horror mounted when he discovered that one of the bodies was that of a boy not much older than Zach. The young Ute was on his stomach, blank eyes wide, tongue lolling. Something had torn his back open from the shoulder blades to the hip, tearing out his spine in the process.

Involuntarily, Nate shivered. Cold fingers rubbed across his skin, or seemed to, and he erupted in goose bumps. Just then a burning branch in the fire crackled loudly, causing him to jump.

Angry at himself, Nate firmed his grip on the Hawken and moved to the middle of the clearing. The bodies he passed all bore similar terrible wounds. One man had no head, and the stump of the warrior's neck bore clear teeth marks. Again Nate leaned down.

Grizzly teeth were broad and strong, designed for crunching. Wolves had teeth capped with sharp points, for cutting. Painter teeth were long and razor sharp, perfect for slicing and shredding. Whatever had slain the Utes had teeth that combined all those traits, and more. They were broad at the base, long and slightly curved, with thin points. A vicious combination, ideal for hooking into prey and ripping it to ribbons.

As Nate straightened, he beheld a clear track, an impression left by the creature responsible in a puddle of blood. His breath caught in his throat. "It can't be!" he exclaimed in a whisper. "It just can't!"

The print was twice as long as his own, longer even than that of a grizzly. But where a grizzly's was broad and flat, this was narrow, exceedingly so. He thought that he could make out the faint outline of a fifth claw, but he could not be sure.

Among the trapping fraternity, Nate was regarded as one of the best trackers. That said a lot, considering that the mountaineers, as they were fond of calling themselves, had to be skilled at reading sign in order to make a living at their trade. Even among the Shoshones, Nate's ability was envied.

Nate could identify any animal by its track. From the smallest to the biggest, from chipmunks to buffalo, he had memorized the traits of each. So it was another jolt to discover that the print in front of him had been left by something totally alien, by an animal he had never encountered, by something out of a lunatic's worst nightmare.

A low groan reached Nate's ears. Whirling, he studied the bodies and was surprised when one feebly twitched—surprised because the Ute in question should, by rights, be dead. The man's torso had been rent every which way. Strands of skin were all that was holding him together.

Nate hurried over. The warrior's eyes were open. A spark of life shone in them as Nate sank onto a knee. "I am a friend," he said in the Ute language. He was not as fluent in it as he was in the Shoshone tongue and several others, but he could get by.

The man's mouth moved. His tongue flicked out, wetting his dry lips. "Grizzly Killer?" he gasped.

The Shoshones, the Flatheads, the Crows, the Utes, all knew Nate by that name. It had been bestowed on him years before by a Cheyenne after Nate barely survived a clash with a fierce silvertip. "I am," the trapper confirmed.

The warrior reached up and weakly gripped Nate's sleeve. "You are friend to Two Owls."

"Yes." Two Owls was an Ute chief Nate had befriended many moons before, and was largely responsible for the current truce.

"I am Red Feather. Remember me?"

Nate's brow furrowed. The man's face was somewhat familiar, now that he thought about it. "Did we meet when I visited Two Owls at his village?" he prompted.

"I am his brother."

It came back to Nate in a rush of vivid memory. Two Owls had four brothers, and one night they had been invited to a feast in his honor. Red Feather had been rather aloof, never saying much. Nate had chalked it up to the abiding mistrust the Utes had for whites in general. "I remember you."

The warrior's fingers dug into the mountain man's brawny arm. "Please, Grizzly Killer. Save him."

"Save who?" Nate replied, thinking the man must be delirious. "I am sorry. The rest of your band are all dead."

"My son. Find him. Take him to Two Owls."

Nate surveyed the clearing once more. No one else showed a trace of life. Red Feather was the sole survivor. "Rest. I will bring water and—"

"No!" the Ute declared, his voice thick with emotion. "Please." With a monumental effort, he rose onto an elbow, clinging to Nate for support. "I saw them take him."

"Who?"

"The others. The People of the Mist."

"I have never heard of a tribe by that name." Nate tried to pry the man's fingers loose so he could gently lower the warrior. It was common knowledge that a person's mind played tricks on them at the end. They saw things that were not there, they heard voices no one else could.

Red Feather would not let go. "Please," he begged yet again, passion restoring some of the color to his cheeks. "Promise me, Grizzly Killer. Promise me you will save Nevava."

Running Fox, Nate mentally translated as he at last succeeded in freeing his arm and slowly eased the Ute to the ground. "Be still, friend. I—"

Desperation lent the distraught father extra strength. Suddenly clawing at Nate's hunting shirt, he practically wailed, "Promise me!"

The heartfelt appeal stirred Nate in the depths of his soul. It was a plea from one warrior to another, from one father to another. "I promise," he pledged. Hardly were the words out of his mouth before Red Feather stiffened, exhaled loudly, then sagged, as limp as a wet rag. The spark of life faded from his eyes, and the last word that passed his lips was the name of his son.

"Nevava."

Nate slowly rose. Plainly, Red Feather had loved his son as much as Nate loved Zach. Mightily moved, he coughed to clear a lump in his throat. "I'll do what I can," he vowed to the corpse. Which might be awfully little. He had no idea who the People of the Mist were, or where to find their territory. Remembering the vague figures spotted earlier, he walked toward the west end of the encampment. A low bank marked the boundary of a shallow stream, its surface shimmering in the sunshine.

A nicker brought Nate up short. He had forgotten about the one he had heard a while before. Southwest of the camp lay more than a dozen horses in the same state as their former owners. Bellies had been cut open, spilling intestines and other organs. Legs had been broken like so much kindling. Throats had been torn apart, drenching the animals and the grass, forming red pools linked by trickling rivulets. Already a legion of flies buzzed thick and heavy, drawn to the feast by an unseen force.

A sorrel still lived. Once it had been a splendid mount. Now its coat had been raked repeatedly by iron claws. Huge jaws had taken enormous bites from its haunches. Crimson froth flecked its mouth, and every breath wheezed from its ruptured lungs like a bellows. Yet it clung tenaciously to life, as did all living things. Its eyes swiveled as the trapper walked over.

Nate could not stand to see the poor horse suffer. It was beyond help, so there was only one thing to do. Sliding a pistol from under his belt, he cocked the flintlock and touched the muzzle to the animal's head.

The horse looked at him. Nate swore that it knew, that

it sensed what he was going to do. It gazed at the blue vault of sky, as if for a last glimpse before the end. When Nate squeezed the trigger, the pistol boomed, spewing smoke and lead. The shot was true.

Sighing, Nate promptly reloaded. It was the first important lesson his mentor, Shakespeare McNair, had taught. Never leave a gun unloaded. To do so invited trouble.

Going to the stream, Nate examined the bank. Fresh footprints were proof that the figures he had glimpsed had indeed crossed and gone to the west. He counted six sets of tracks, five belonging to grown men, one set belonging to a boy of ten or twelve.

"Nevava," Nate said aloud. Evidently Red Feather had not been delirious. The People of the Mist, whoever they were, had taken the Ute's son. Nate pondered, wondering what link, if any, there was between the mysterious new tribe and the calamity that befell the hunting party. The grotesque tracks, the claw and teeth marks, they all pointed to an unknown creature of incredible size and power. Could it be a beast under their control? The notion seemed far-fetched. But another lesson Nate had learned was to never take anything for granted.

A hint of movement brought Nate around in a twinkling. Winona, Evelyn, and Zach were crossing the clearing, the three of them in a collective daze.

Winona could not believe what she was seeing. This was worse than the time the Blackfeet massacred a band of her people, worse than the havoc wrought by a rampaging grizzly. She held Evelyn close to her bosom so the girl could not see the worst of it.

Zach was flabbergasted. In his short life he had tangled with bears, buffalo, and wolverines. He had fought Piegans, Bloods, and murderous whites. He had seen plenty of dead people, but nothing to match this. Coming on a track of the brute responsible, he gawked in mingled awe and dread. What sort of monster could do such a thing? he asked himself.

Evelyn was glad her mother had averted her face. The sickening scene had made her queasy. One warrior in particular. He had been shorn nearly in half, the upper part of his body connected to the lower section by a strip of flesh barely as wide as her hand.

"What are you doing here?" Nate demanded. "I told you to stay put."

"We heard a shot," Winona answered absently, distracted by the slaughter. "What happened to these men, husband?"

"I don't rightly know," Nate admitted. Briefly, he related the sequence of events, concluding with "I've always been a man of my word. Which means I'm obligated to honor my pledge to Red Feather."

"Fine by me, Pa," Zach said, excited at the prospect of counting coup on Nevava's abductors. Equally thrilling was the possibility of killing whatever had wiped out the Utes. His standing among the Shoshones would rise immensely. "When do we start?"

"We?" Nate repeated. "I'm the one going after the boy. You and your mother will return to our cabin."

Winona and Zachary both said "No!" simultaneously. Mother and son swapped glances, then Winona took a step forward, saying, "You would abandon us here? What if more People of the Mist are in this area?"

"Or the critter that tore this bunch to shreds?" Zach interjected, upset that his father would even think of denying them the right to go along. Fate had given them a golden chance to reap untold glory. They would be fools to waste it.

Nate had anticipated objections and was set to stand firm, but he hesitated, bothered by the truth of their assertions. No matter what he did, he was taking a gamble. So what if the tracks of the People of the Mist and those of the creature pointed westward. "I guess the only thing for me to do is to take all of you home, then come back alone."

"It would take over half a moon," Winona said. "The trail would be cold by then." Something else occurred to her. "Afternoon thunderstorms are common this time of year. One might erase the tracks." Shaking her head, she stated, "To save the boy, we must go on now. Together. As a family. As we always do."

"I agree with Ma," Zach said, just to throw in his two bits' worth.

Evelyn did not comment. Being the youngest, she was used to not having her opinion asked, so she seldom gave it. If someone *had* asked, though, she would have told them that she would rather be with both her folks—and, yes, even with her rascally brother—than anywhere else.

Affection and common sense waged a war in Nate King's heart, and affection won. It would always win. For the mountain man was not one of those who could easily turn his back on those he cared for most in the world.

He had known men like that back in New York City and elsewhere. Coldhearted husbands who could go off carousing at cards or frolicking with tavern wenches for days on end, with nary a twinge of regret. Men who would up and cut out whenever the mood was right, not caring one whit how their families fared while they were gone.

"A strong family, a family that endures, is one that sticks together through thick and thin." Those were his very words, expressed on a number of occasions.

So now Nate King swallowed hard, prayed he was not making the worst mistake of his life, and announced, "I know when I'm licked. We'll cut out after the People of the Mist and try to catch them before they get very far."

Only Zach whooped for joy.

Chapter Three

The farther they went, the more mystified Nate King grew.

When it became apparent that the People of the Mist did not have horses hidden near the camp and were traveling on foot, Nate waxed confident that he would overtake them quickly. Two days at the most, he figured. But the mysterious warriors held to a pace few could rival. Not only that, they always stuck to the roughest terrain; picking a route that taxed horses to the limit. Nearly impassable timber, the steepest of slopes, over ravines and through gorges, the People of the Mist did not miss a trick.

It had to be intentional, Nate decided. Either they knew they were being followed, which was highly unlikely, or they had developed the habit of always making it ungodly hard for possible enemies to shadow them.

If they were that wary, it might explain why few tribes had ever heard of them. Nate found it mighty strange that no one had mentioned them before. At one time or another he had visited every friendly tribe within four hundred miles of his homestead, yet not once had anyone alluded to the People of the Mist.

It was all the more strange when he considered that Indians had refined conversation to a fine art. They liked nothing better than to sit around a toasty fire in the evening swapping stories. Accounts of battles, coups earned, heroic deeds, tragedies that befell hapless individuals, anything and everything was ripe to be discussed. Unusual happenings were a favorite topic. So why, then, had no one ever brought up this mysterious new tribe?

The small band was on a beeline to the southwest. Adding to the mystery was the fact that the creature responsible for making worm food of the Utes was *also* heading to the southwest. It could not be mere happenstance.

The tracks of the People of the Mist and the creature often overlapped, and Nate could not determine if the People of the Mist were following the creature or if the creature was following them.

Yet another curious aspect were the footprints of the warriors. As every frontiersman was aware, no two tribes fashioned their moccasins exactly alike. Usually it was possible to peg the makers of any set of tracks by the characteristics of the prints. The Arapahos, for instance, favored broad-soled footwear, while the Sioux went in for soles with narrow toes and heels.

The prints of the People of the Mist showed that they wore moccasins totally different from any other, but oddly so. The soles were narrow their entire length, which told him that the warriors had extremely narrow feet. In addition, the soles left odd circular impressions every few inches along the outer edge, as if they had knobs of some sort on the bottom. Which made no sense.

As for the creature, it held to the same tireless pace as

the People of the Mist. Several times, where it crossed soft earth, Nate discovered a long furrow. At first he thought the creature must be dragging something. Then the truth hit him. The thing had a tail, a *big* tail.

It was conclusive evidence, as if any more were needed, that the beast was a monstrosity, so out of the ordinary, so different from the wildlife Nate was accustomed to, that he could not begin to guess what it might be.

Five days passed. Five days of hard riding, of being in the saddle from sunup to sunset, of spending restless nights and having to make do with pemmican and jerky instead of freshly killed game.

Nate was used to such hardship. Working a trapline year in and year out for over a decade had tempered his muscles into living steel and rendered his will as rock-hard as his whipcord body.

Trapping was not for the weak or the timid. A man had to go off into country rife with hostile Indians and roving predators. He had to contend with the worst of weather. With bitter wind and stinging cold. With water so frigid that standing in it too long induced frostbite, which might end up costing a few toes or part of a foot.

His days were spent slogging through creeks and rivers to set half a dozen traps, or to check on those previously placed. Doing so in itself was a chore. A trapper had to locate a choice spot, then pry the jagged jaws of a trap apart, carefully set them, and just as carefully lower the trap under the surface. The idea was for the beaver to mosey along, catch a whiff of the castorium that the trapper applied to a leaf or twig above the trap, and blunder into it.

Then came the really hard part. The trapper had to lift the heavy beaver out. Considering that most of the critters weighed upward of fifty pounds, that they were waterlogged and mired fast in the steel jaws of the

Newhouse, a day's work often left a trapper so exhausted that he eagerly crawled under the covers as soon as the sun went down, only to wake up at the crack of dawn to repeat the whole ordeal all over again.

No, trapping was not for the puny. Thanks to his years of toil, Nate could endure hardships most men could not. Picture the harshest of conditions, and he had survived them. He could go for days with little food or rest, and often had.

So the pursuit of the People of the Mist did not bother him in the least. But his family was another matter. Winona had demonstrated time and again that she could hold her own under the worst of circumstances, and Zach was willing to endure any hardship to prove he was becoming a man. But Evelyn, tiny Evelyn, had never gone this long with so little rest and nourishment.

Nate fretted about her constantly. He saw the weariness in her face, and he admired how she gamely rode on, mile after mile, day after day, without complaint, although she was so stiff and sore that in the evening she grimaced whenever she stood up or sat down.

After five days, Nate was inclined to call it quits. He had done his best, but the People of the Mist were too crafty. Catching them would take much longer than he had anticipated. His daughter was at the limit of her endurance, and the horses were flagging.

One more day, Nate told himself. He would give it another twenty-four hours, and if fortune did not smile on them, if they did not catch sight of a campfire or the People of the Mist themselves, he would recommend that they turn around and head home.

Promise or no promise, Nate would not put any of his family at risk. Evelyn's health was more important than his word.

Then came the sixth day. It dawned crisp and clear, as had the others. The morning was spent winding down a series of heavily forested slopes, which was no different from their activity on any other day.

But along about noon, as they neared the bottom of a slope, the pines thinned, then abruptly ended. Before their wondering eyes unfolded a startling vista of arid buttes and mesas and canyons. Hardly a tree grew anywhere. The scant grass was dry and withered. A few stunted shrubs had managed to take root here and there. It was a desolate wasteland, normally shunned by whites and Indians alike.

Yet to Nate's amazement, the tracks of the People of the Mist *and* those of the creature had trekked off across it, into the heart of the foreboding unknown. Reining up, he rose in the stirrups. Nothing moved out there, not so much as a bird or a lizard. "I don't like it," he announced.

"We cannot stop," Winona said. "Think of the Ute boy." Unslinging the water skin from her saddle, she opened it and held it out for Evelyn to take a drink.

"I'm thinking of us," Nate responded, grimly surveying the desolation. There was hardly any cover. If they were caught in the open, they could be picked off one by one.

Zach fidgeted and hefted his Hawken. "I don't mind going on if Ma doesn't," he commented, afraid his chance to count coup was slipping away. Each day he grew more and more impatient to catch the other party.

Evelyn grinned at her father. "It's fine by me, Pa," she chimed in.

Always the sunny one, Nate mused. *Always ready to do her part.* "Thank you, princess." He fibbed to spare her feelings. "But it's the horses I'm concerned about. They're tuckered out. And from the look of things, finding water from here on out will be like pulling a hen's teeth."

Giggling, Evelyn said, "Pa, chickens don't have teeth. Even I know that."

Nate faced his wife. "We can rest here until morning, then head back. What do you say?"

"I have already told you. There is the boy to think of. Would you give up if it were Stalking Coyote or Blue Flower? No, of course not. We must go on." Winona held up a hand when Nate opened his mouth to speak. "I know what you will say. You are concerned about us. You do not want us to be harmed. I share your sentiments, husband, but I will not let them stop us from doing what is right. No one else knows the Ute boy was taken captive. Unless we save him, his fate is sealed." She paused. "Is that the right expression?"

Nate nodded, peeved that once again she was relying on pure logic to thwart his wishes. Women were like that. Whether red or white, they always gave the impression of being highly emotional, of wearing their hearts on their sleeves, as it were. But the truth was that they had minds like steel traps. Deep down, they were as logical as men. No, they were more so—as any married man would confirm.

"Then we're pushing on?" Zach asked. In his mind's eye he saw himself riding into the village of his mother's people, new scalps slung across his horse for everyone to admire. Or else with the hide of the strange creature wrapped around his shoulders like a royal robe. Wouldn't that impress the Shoshones no end!

"We are," Winona said, clucking to her mare before Nate could object. Yes, she sincerely appreciated his devotion. But she would not allow him to compromise his ideals for their sakes.

Of all the men she had ever met, Nathaniel King was one of the most noble. No one had been more shocked than she when she realized she was falling in love with him. How ironic, in light of the interest in her by virtually every unattached warrior in her village. She had been the one woman they most wanted, the "prize catch," as Nate once phrased it.

And she picked a white man.

Small wonder hard feelings resulted, and a leading warrior later tried to tear her from Nate against her will.

Winona dispelled the bitter memory with a toss of her head. She had no regrets over her decision. Nate was the one for her, the "love as deep as a chasm, as wide as the heavens" her mother had always talked about.

That they were husband and wife was a minor miracle. They had been drawn together over vast gulfs, gulfs they had to surmount in order to be united. A race gulf, a culture gulf, a gulf of many miles.

She was proud of her man. Proud of his love for her, of his love for their children, of the hard work he did to provide for them. She was most proud that he was not like some other husbands she had heard about. Men who treated their women worse than they treated their horse or their dog.

Nate had always treated her with the utmost respect. True, they had spats from time to time, but he never ranted and raved, never tried to "put her in her proper place," as the husband of a cousin always did. He regarded her as an equal partner and valued her insights. What more could any woman ask of a man?

The clatter of hooves alongside the mare brought an end to Winona's reverie. "Are you mad at me?" she bluntly asked.

"I just hope you're right," Nate answered with a meaningful look at their daughter and son.

"We are doing what we must. Come what may, my love, we will live by our decision and accept the consequences."

As he had so many times in the past, Nate marveled at her command of English. He could speak Shoshone, but nowhere near as eloquently as she did his language. Part of her mastery, he suspected, stemmed from the small library he had painstakingly collected, books by James Fenimore Cooper and others, each as precious as gold.

Nate had always loved to read. It inspired him, transported his imagination to places he had never been, taught him about aspects of life he otherwise might not have paid attention to. Cooper, Scott, Byron, Shakespeare, they all had something to impart, and impart they did, each and every night. It was a family custom that after the evening meal he would read aloud for half an hour or more.

Naturally, Winona had picked up words even most trappers rarely used. Shakespeare McNair liked to say that listening to her was the next best thing to reading the bard, a high tribute from a man whose fondness for the English playwright had earned him his nickname.

"Pa, what's that up ahead?"

Zach's query made Nate realize that he had let his mind stray, a dangerous practice in a land where death struck fast and furious, without warning. Ahead was a bluff. A hundred yards to the north of it, prone in the dust, was a reddish object. It was not a plant, not a rock. Another twenty yards and Nate recognized outspread limbs and the outline of a human head. "Hold up," he directed.

Spurring the stallion, Nate moved in for a closer look. After the carnage at the clearing, he knew what to expect. The stink of rotting flesh was awful. It unnerved the stallion. The horse balked, and he had to goad it onward.

A halo of dry blood framed the victim's head. Half the flesh was gone from his rib cage. So was most of his right thigh. Something had feasted well at his expense.

The stallion grew more agitated. So much so that Nate drew rein, slid off, and continued on foot.

The Lost Valley

At last he had found one of the People of the Mist. The man was tall and lean in build. A hawkish nose dominated a pear-shaped face with high cheekbones, a firm mouth, and a strong jawbone. The hair hung loose, falling past his shoulders at the back but clipped just below his ears on the sides and just above his eyebrows in front.

His clothes consisted of a long-sleeved shirt, baggy pants, high moccasins with quilled heel straps, and a wide headband similar to those Nate had seen worn by Apaches. Around his neck was a bear-claw necklace. No weapons were on him, but it was evident he had sold his life dearly. His torn shirt and pants were soaked with blood. On his forearms were many bite marks.

Nate inspected the moccasins. Thick leather cord had been used to sew on the soles. Every few inches along the edge the cord had been knotted, which accounted for the unusual impressions Nate had observed in the tracks.

It was no mystery what had slain the man. Dotting the bare earth were more of the gigantic tracks Nate had been following for days. He backtracked, reading the spoor as he might read print in a book.

Apparently the creature had been ahead of the warriors all along. Either it had stopped to rest in the shadows at the base, or it had deliberately lurked there, waiting for them to catch up. The onslaught had been swift, catching them off guard. They had scattered, but the victim had not been quick enough. He had paid with his life.

Nate hunkered beside a perfect set of huge prints. "What in the world are you?" he said uneasily. The Utes, the People of the Mist, no one was able to stop it. He lowered a hand to run a finger over a claw mark.

"Pa! Look out!"

Zach's cry snapped Nate erect. From out of the shadows had hurtled another warrior, a war club upraised to strike.

Chapter Four

Nate King brought up the Hawken just in time to block the blow. The impact jolted him backward, and his right foot snagged on the dead man. He lost his balance and fell, landing on his back. The club arced down again, but Nate rolled to the left and heard it thud into the corpse. Dimly, he was aware of Winona, Zach, and Evelyn flying to his aid. He had to dispatch his attacker before they were close enough to be harmed.

Surging onto his knees, Nate warded off another blow. Briefly, the club and the rifle barrel locked together. He saw that it was a type of club foreign to him, different from those used by the Blackfeet, the Crows, and the Shoshones. This was a curved affair about as long as a man's arm, pale brown except for black ritual markings, with thin edges for hacking rather than bashing.

The warrior holding it had the same size and build as the dead man. His clothes were the same style, only his shirt was red and he did not wear a bear-claw necklace.

His face was not as broad, his eyes aglow with battle lust.

With a wrench the warrior tore the club free. Sidestepping, he sheared it at Nate's neck. Nate countered, but the rifle was jarred from his grasp when the warrior jerked the club to the right. In sheer reflex Nate threw himself at the man's legs, tackling him. Nate brought the warrior crashing down and quickly scrambled onto the man's chest to pin him. But the warrior was as strong as a panther and as slippery as a wet weasel. Bucking upward, he dislodged Nate, then twisted and swung the club.

Nate whipped both arms up, catching hold of the man's wrist a split second before the club could connect. Grappling, they rose onto their knees. Nate was bigger and heavier and more powerful across the shoulders. Gradually, he forced the man back, bending him nearly in half. Sweat broke out on the warrior's forehead and he sputtered from his herculean effort, but he could not tear loose, could not bring the club to bear.

Unexpectedly shifting, Nate shoved the warrior onto his back and flung his body across the man's upper torso and arms. Now the warrior *was* pinned. He heaved and thrashed, but Nate held on fast.

"Give up," the mountain man said. "I don't want to harm you if I can avoid it."

Evidently the warrior did not understand English. He renewed his struggles, and had nearly succeeded in slipping out from underneath when a rifle barrel flashed out of nowhere and jammed against his cheek. The warrior froze.

"Want me to shoot him for you, Pa?" Zach asked eagerly, thinking how great the man's hair would look hanging from a coup stick.

Nate glanced up, appalled by the blood lust his son's expression registered. Something was happening to his son, something he did not like. They needed to sit down and have a long heart-to-heart talk. But this was hardly the right time or place. "No," he said sternly. "He's not our enemy."

Winona stepped into view, her rifle leveled. The warrior saw her and his brow knit. He said a few words in a tongue she did not understand. She shook her head to signify as much, and he frowned in disappointment.

Nate slowly rose, yanking the club from the man's grip. It was surprisingly light in weight. Casting it aside, he drew a flintlock and moved several strides back. "Let's try to communicate with him," he proposed.

The warrior sat up, glanced sadly at his slain companion, then rested his arms on his knees and clamped his mouth in sullen defiance.

"Do you savvy my language?" Nate asked. Eliciting no reaction, he reverted to Shoshone, asking the same question. He tried the Flathead tongue, the Crow. Tucking the pistol under an arm, he employed sign language. It was his last resort, and he was highly hopeful it would work. Nearly every tribe knew sign. At least, those who dwelled on the plains and in the eastern half of the Rockies did. During his trek to the Pacific Ocean he had learned that many in the far northwest woods did not.

The warrior stared blankly as the trapper's fingers weaved patterns in the air.

"He doesn't savyy, Pa," Zach noted the obvious. "Or else he's faking it."

"Why would he?" Nate held the pistol and mulled over what to do next. Squatting, he pointed at the warrior, then drew a crude outline of a human figure in the dirt. Pointing at the dead man, he did the same. Next he drew three more, one for each of the other members of the band. Finally, he drew a small boy and looked expectantly at their captive.

The warrior stared at the drawings, at Nate. He spoke

at length. When Nate shook his head and shrugged, the warrior jabbed a finger westward a few times, said a few words, then drew a rectangular shape in the dirt with what appeared to be a door at the bottom.

Nate gathered that the man had told him the boy was being taken to their village. But the shape of the structure was puzzling. Most Indian lodges were either conical tepees or domelike wigwams. "How far?" he asked, forgetting himself. To demonstrate, he pointed at the sun and swept his arm across the sky from east to west.

The warrior caught on right away. He made three sweeps, then raised his arm from the eastern horizon to midway in the sky.

"Three and a half days is not much," Winona said. "We have come this far. We should see it through."

"I could go on alone from here," Nate offered, knowing full well he was wasting his breath. "You can wait back up in the trees by the last stream we passed. It would take a load off my mind knowing you were safe."

"Where you go, my husband, we all go."

There were occasions, Nate reflected, when women were the most exasperating creatures on God's green earth. They were willing to abide by logic only when it was *their* logic that was being followed. And they had the gall to call men stubborn!

Turning to the warrior, Nate touched his own chest and said his name several times. He indicated each member of his family and did likewise. When he was done, he pointed at the man and waited.

"Pahchatka," the warrior declared, smacking his sternum.

It was a crucial moment. Their captive had grown more at ease once it dawned on him that they were not going to kill him outright. Now Nate picked up the war club and handed it to him.

Pahchatka could not hide his astonishment. Accepting

37

the weapon, he studied each of them in turn, focusing at last on Nate. His mouth curled upward. He put a finger on his chest and drew the outline of a heart, then closed his fingers around the imaginary organ.

"Lower your guns," Nate directed, doing so himself. Wedging the flintlock under his belt, he extended an arm. Pahchatka looked at his hand a few moments, then gripped it and let himself be hauled erect. Nate reclaimed his rifle, contriving not to turn his back just in case he had misjudged.

Winona did as her husband bid, but she was nervous about arming the warrior when their children were so near. To be safe, she did not let down the hammer, and she made a mental note to never let the man out of her sight.

Zach was fit to be tied. They had wasted an ideal opportunity to count coup. It aggravated him that his father was being so friendly. That did not bode well for the future, when they caught up with those who had stolen the Ute boy. Based on the overtures his pa had made, they would attempt to get the boy back without bloodshed—without counting coup.

"Son, fetch the horses," Nate instructed. As Zach ran off, Nate moved to where prints of the mystery beast had not been trampled in their struggle. Dipping a toe onto one, he said, "What is this critter?" accenting his question with an arch of his eyebrows.

Pahchatka grew somber. "Kachina," he said, and to Nate's amazement, he trembled slightly from head to toe.

Nate sorely desired to learn more, but the language barrier handicapped him. "How big is it?" he inquired. Naturally, the warrior regarded him quizzically, so Nate held his hands at arm's length to suggest size.

Comprehending immediately, Pahchatka walked a few yards and scraped a short furrow with the tip of his club. Pivoting, he took ten precise paces to the north, then scraped another furrow. Swinging around, he held out his arms as Nate had done.

"Impossible," Nate said. Yet he could not deny the evidence of his own eyes. The tracks hinted at immense bulk; now Pahchatka had confirmed it. But *thirty feet*? That was four times the length of a grizzly, three times the size of a bull buffalo. And what was he to make of the long tail? "What kind of monster are we dealing with?" he breathed.

"Maybe it is something from the Old Time," Winona said.

"The what?"

"The time when Coyote and his woman gave birth to the first people. The time when many strange things roamed the land."

Nate was familiar with the Shoshone account of Creation, and their belief in the hereafter. Initially, it had surprised him to learn they had a strong belief in life after death. Most whites branded them as heathens, little better than animals, a prejudice that had tainted his outlook until he learned differently.

According to their legends, the father of their people was called Coyote, the Trickster. But the two branches of the Shoshones could not agree on exactly how Coyote brought them into being.

The Shoshones who lived west of the Rockies, called "Diggers" by the mountain men, believed that in ages past Coyote formed the first man and woman from clay, then breathed life into them.

The Shoshones who lived in the mountains, Winona's people, held that Coyote had married a wild woman who killed and ate anyone who came to her lodge. By the power of the special blue stone Coyote always carried, he tamed this wild girl, and the fruits of their union brought into being the firstborn of all the tribes in the world.

David Thompson

The Shoshones had other tales of those ancient times. Tales no sane man would credit. Tales of beasts with skin as thick as a knight's armor, of birds without feathers that had wingspans wide enough to blot out the sun, of shaggy animals twice as big as buffalo but with shiny tusks instead of black horns and noses like writhing snakes.

There were other things. Horrid things, things the Shoshones talked about only in whispers and never in the presence of children.

Was this one? Nate wondered as Pahchatka walked toward them. Could it be possible that some of the old tales had a basis in fact? He dismissed the notion for the time being and set about learning something else. Pinching his cheek, he said, "White man," over and over. Then, going to his wife, he rubbed her cheek, saying, "Shoshone."

For once Pahchatka was at a loss. Nate had to repeat himself several times, then point at the sun, at the bluff, and at a rock, and say each of their names, before the warrior grinned and declared proudly while pinching his own cheek, "Anasazi."

Nate had never heard of them, but then, he had never heard of the Chinooks, the Spokans, or the Wenatchis before his trek to the Pacific with Shakespeare McNair. McNair claimed there were scores of isolated tribes scattered in regions so remote that no white man had ever visited them. The Anasazis must be one of them.

At that juncture Zach arrived, leading the four horses.

Evelyn mounted without being told to do so. She had not uttered a word since the warrior attacked her father, and she did not feel comfortable around him. Secretly, she wished the man would go away, but she trusted her parents enough to go along with whatever they wanted.

Nate mounted last. He offered a hand to the Anasazi so they could ride double. But Pahchatka recoiled as if

40

he had been slapped. Nate beckoned, smiling to show his peaceful intentions. To no avail. The warrior motioned sharply, refusing. Nate reined the stallion toward him and was stunned when Pahchatka frantically bounded to the west a dozen feet. "What in the world?"

"He is scared of horses," Winona guessed. From her grandfather she had heard of those days long past when her own people first set eyes on them, and the terror horses had inspired. A band of Shoshones had been hunting buffalo far to the south of their usual haunts when they met up with a group of mounted Comanches. While not strictly allies, in the old days the two tribes had traded on occasion. Her grandfather loved to tell of the return of the hunters with two of the wondrous beasts, and the widespread panic it caused. She could remember the wizened oldster laughing uproariously as he related how women screamed and scooped up their bawling children and fled into their lodges, while warriors milled in numb panic.

"How can that be?" Nate was saying. "He must have seen them before. There were horses at the Ute camp."

"But perhaps he does not know what they are."

Nate tried once more. Climbing down, he stroked the stallion to show how tame it was, then smiled and gestured for the Anasazi to do likewise. Pahchatka would have none of it. Muttering, the warrior made repeated signs in the air, as if warding off evil.

Recognizing a lost cause, Nate swung back on and was set to ride off when the reek of the rotting body reminded him of an oversight. Nodding at it, he looked at Pahchatka and gestured as if to say, "What should we do with him?"

The warrior tilted an arm to the heavens. Half a dozen vultures had assembled. Soon more would arrive, and by sunset of the next day the dead man's bones would be virtually stripped bare.

Once Nate would have been incensed by the idea of leaving a man to be consumed by the ugly carrion eaters. That was before he traveled west, before he learned—the hard way—that life in the wild was a never-ending test of wit and brawn, and those who failed the test were seldom given the luxury of a decent burial. As his mentor had once put it, "Dead is dead, young coon. It doesn't make a lick of difference to a lifeless husk if worms and maggots consume it, or if it ends up as what comes out of a buzzard's butt." Crude, yet oh so true.

Pahchatka broke into a steady jog he maintained for hours at a stretch, far longer than Nate could have done. The only other warriors able to duplicate the feat, to his knowledge, were Apaches.

The countryside grew more arid the farther they went. No grass grew, and the stunted bushes vanished. Clouds of dust rose from under the hooves of the horses, clinging to them, getting into their hair, their eyes, even under their clothes.

They never lacked for water. Pahchatka seemed to know where every spring and tank was and arranged it so that each evening they bedded down with a source of refreshing water nearby. For supper they ate roasted lizard or snake, usually caught by the Anasazi.

For four nights and three days they paralleled the tracks of Nevava's abductors. On the fourth morning they were awakened before sunrise by an excited Pahchatka. He insisted they push on right away. It soon became apparent why.

Directly to the west reared a towering mesa. They had first seen it about noon the day before, a reddish stump in the distance that grew and grew and grew. Now, in the pale light of false dawn, Nate was startled to see that the entire lower half of the escarpment was sheathed in a swirling, shimmering mist. "The People of the Mist," he said, understanding what Red Feather had meant at last.

As if in answer, from out of the thick veil wavered a piercing howl.

Chapter Five

The Anasazi drew up short and cocked his head, listening to another howl that rose to a inhuman crescendo, then tapered. Pahchatka hefted his war club and glanced at Nate and Winona. Baring his teeth as would a savage beast, he made slashing movements with his left hand.

His message was clear. Whatever lurked in the mist was dangerous. Nate pointed at the eastern horizon, where a pink tinge heralded a new day. He was content to stay where they were until the sun had risen and burned the mist off. When the Anasazi resumed walking, Nate called his name. Pahchatka watched intently as Nate sought to explain, using hand gestures.

The warrior pointed at the sun, then at the mist. He held his hand at shoulder height and lowered it several times, always stopping at his knees.

Nate was perplexed and looked at Winona. "Do you savvy what he's trying to tell us?"

"No."

44

Again Pahchatka went through his pantomime, only this time he would point at the sun and sweep his arm a bit higher before he held his hand flat and lowered it by degrees until it was at his knees again.

"Beats me all hollow," Nate said.

"Me too, Pa," Zach said. He would never admit as much, but the howls had unnerved him. They were different from those of wolves or coyotes. They were louder, throatier, ripe with menace. Deep inside, they provoked a twinge of unreasoning fear, similar to the fear he'd had of the dark when he was barely old enough to walk. He felt ashamed.

Winona stared thoughtfully at the roiling wall of mist. "I think I have it figured out," she told her husband. "He is telling us that even after the sun rises, the mist never goes completely away."

"Impossible," Nate said. Many a fine morning high in the mountains he had come out of their cabin to see their valley shrouded in mist or fog, but neither ever lasted long. Heat from the rising sun always evaporated them, just as it did the dew that moistened the grass.

Pahchatka said a few words, then moved on, stalking forward like a cat, poised on the balls of his feet, his war club ready to swing.

Nate did not like it one bit. Fighting wild animals he was familiar with was one thing. But the beasts in the mist were as mysterious as the giant creature that had wiped out the Utes. He had no inkling of how big they were, or how strong, or how fierce, and being ignorant of their nature could prove fatal.

A man not only had to know the habits of the wildlife he shared the wilderness with, he had to learn their weaknesses, as well. Many a young would-be trapper, on being charged by a grizzly for the first time, had discovered to his dismay that shooting a grizzly in the head was a waste of lead. So massive were their skulls that bullets invariably glanced off. A grizzly's sole weak spot was behind its humped shoulders, halfway down its body. A ball there stood a good chance of hitting its heart or lungs.

Pahchatka had stopped and was waving them on. Nate hesitated, unwilling to expose his loved ones to unknown peril. If the Anasazi was right about the mist always being there, it made no difference whether they went in now or waited until sunrise. But he could not, in good conscience, lead them farther.

Winona sensed her husband's turmoil. It pleased her that he always thought of their welfare before all else. Unfortunately, sometimes he was too protective. It was wrong of her, she knew, but she could not help feeling that he did not think she was competent enough to deal with whatever situations might arise. And no woman liked for her man to think she could not hold her own. "Keep going," she said. "We have come too far to turn back."

Against his better judgment, Nate clucked to the stallion. No more howls broke the eerie stillness as they neared the shimmering wall, which in itself was profoundly unsettling. A whitish gray, it roiled and writhed as if alive. The Anasazi halted fifteen feet out, squatted, and peered into the veil.

Nate could not see a thing. Up close, the mist was composed of wispy tendrils, always in motion, vaporous snakes that ceaselessly entwined among one another. "Hold on," he said when Pahchatka rose, and the warrior looked back.

Reaching into a parfleche, Nate pulled out a coiled rope. Ordinarily it was for tethering the horses at night. Wheeling the stallion, he moved down the line and gave one end to Zach. "Whatever you do, don't let go,"

"Don't worry, Pa." Zach bent his neck to gaze at the top of the shimmering barrier. It had to be two hundred feet high. Above the mist reared the mesa, a sheer rock wall that gave the illusion of stretching to the clouds. Zach could not say why, but a tremor rippled through his body.

Nate turned the stallion and rode to his daughter, uncoiling the rope as he went along. She smiled at him in her innocent, trusting manner when he came alongside her pony. "Hold up your arms," he said. After she did, he looped the rope once around her waist. "It's so we won't get separated."

"This should be fun," Evelyn said. "It'll be like riding in fog." Sometimes, when her mother took her for morning rides along the shore of the lake near their homestead, they would dash through lingering patches.

"Keep your eyes skinned," Nate advised.

"For what? Those wolves? They don't scare me." Evelyn had seen wolves plenty of times and they had never given her any trouble. Her brother had even raised a wolf cub once. When it grew up, it had gone off to be with its own kind. But she could fondly recall many a winter's evening spent lying on the soft bear rug in front of the fireplace with the wolf snuggled at her side. Blaze, as they called him, had often licked her face and hands, making her giggle. She missed him.

Nate tousled Evelyn's hair and moved to Winona. Bending to lightly kiss her cheek, he whispered, "Watch our little muffin like a hawk."

"Would I do otherwise?" Winona said, taking hold of the rope.

It struck Nate that she was miffed at him, but he did not know why. "We'll keep the horses close together, nose to tail," he stated loudly for the benefit of the rest, and wagged the other end of the rope at the Anasazi.

Pahchatka accepted it, then immediately strode into the mist.

The black stallion pricked its ears. It had heard some-

47

thing in there, something that caused it to prance skittishly. "Steady, big fella," Nate said, patting its neck as he followed the warrior.

Evelyn had been right. Entering the mist was like entering a fog bank. The tendrils were cool, moist, and clinging. Nate swatted a hand at some in front of his face and they parted, only to re-form the very next instant. Swiveling, he could barely see Winona, and absolutely nothing of Evelyn or Zach. "Damn," he swore softly. If something attacked, it would be on them before he could lift a finger.

Nate was at a loss to guess how Pahchatka found his way. The Anasazi traveled unerringly onward, never once faltering or stopping, as sure of himself as would be a person out for a Sunday stroll in a park in New York City.

Winona was equally puzzled, and apprehensive. They had not gone far when a breeze sprang up, faint at first but growing stronger. It was a warm breeze, warm yet oddly dank and strangely sweet, like the smell of a field of flowers on a hot summer's day. She twisted to keep an eye on Blue Flower, whispering, "Are you all right back there?"

"Just fine, Ma."

"And you, Stalking Coyote?"

"Don't worry about me. I can take care of myself," Zach said. Although, truth to tell, he was a bundle of nerves. Being swallowed by the mist was an uncomfortable sensation. He could not see more than an arm's length in any direction, and a warrior could not shoot what he could not see. A soft patter to his left startled him. Was it his imagination, or stealthy footsteps? He opened his mouth to warn his parents, then changed his mind. If it was his imagination, his folks would think he was just plain scared. He couldn't have that.

Nate King became aware of a soft, intermittent sighing

up ahead. He strained his ears to identify the sound but could not. Rustling to his left almost made him rein up. Something was out there, shadowing them. He heard the rasp of claws on stone, heard a low growl that was echoed by another on his right.

"Pahchatka!" Nate whispered. Receiving no response, he twisted to signal his wife. She had her rifle up, pointed into the mist. "See anything?"

Winona shook her head. And even as she did, an indistinct shape materialized, a shadowy specter that was there one moment, gone the next. The glimpse was too fleeting for her to make out what it was.

"Ma?" Evelyn said. She had seen the creature, too. It looked like a wolf to her, a really big wolf. She wished Blaze were there to protect them.

Zach brought his Hawken to his shoulder. His father had taught him never to shoot unless he had a clear target, but he was sorely tempted to fire blindly into the gloom. Twice he had seen a shaggy *thing* flanking them.

Suddenly a bloodcurdling howl rent the mist. Without thinking, Nate reined up. The rope grew taut, then went slack, and he feared that it had slipped from Pahchatka's hand. But in a few seconds the warrior appeared beside the stallion and stabbed a finger at various points in the mist. Each time he did, he said, "Nasci."

Nate reckoned it was the Anasazi name for whatever was stalking them. To defend themselves, they must get out of the mist quickly. To that end, he motioned for the warrior to go on. Pahchatka gripped the end of the rope more securely, then hustled forward.

On both sides snarls broke out, so many that Nate could not count them all, drowning the clomp of the stallion's heavy hooves. The beasts were working themselves into a killing frenzy, girding themselves for a concerted rush.

A rumbling growl from the rear was the signal for hell

to break loose. Zach shifted, saw a squat form streak toward his horse, and fired. Whether he hit the thing or not he could not say. At the booming retort it veered off and was engulfed by the mist.

Winona saw one coming toward her. She noticed a beetling brow and a long snout rimmed at the bottom by wicked teeth. Reddish-brown hair covered its face and neck, and there were longer, darker tufts on its throat and shoulders. Splayed paws capped by curved claws dug at the earth. The beast was almost on her when she stroked the trigger.

Momentum carried the thing forward even though its front legs buckled. Sliding to a stop close to the mare, the creature looked up.

It was like a wolf, and yet not like a wolf. Bigger, brawnier, hairier, it had uncommonly wide ears and exceptionally thin legs. A feral gleam lit its dark eyes as it snarled and heaved upward at the mare's jugular. Winona flung back her arms to club it, but she was much too slow.

Nate's rifle cracked just as the nasci's steely jaws were about to crunch shut. It was smashed to the ground, but it did not stay down. With two balls in its body, the creature scrambled erect and plunged into the mist. In its wake rose a chorus of horrendous howls.

Whipping out a pistol, Nate braced for the second wave. Abruptly, unaccountably, the yowling ceased. Total silence reigned—silence more nerve-racking than the howling had been, because Nate knew the things were still out there, standing just beyond the limits of his vision.

Out of the wispy soup appeared Pahchatka, urgently beckoning.

Winona reloaded as they moved on. Slowing so her mare was abreast of Evelyn's pony, she smiled encouragement. Evelyn returned the favor, remarking, "Don't fret, Ma. We can lick these varmints."

Zach drew a flintlock rather than reload his Hawken. He nudged the bay forward so he was close enough to reach out and touch his mother and sister. Come what may, he would protect both with his life, if need be.

The sighing had grown louder. Nate linked it to the breeze, which was stronger whenever the sound increased. The dank scent filled his nostrils, so potent it was like sniffing a pile of freshly dug dirt.

After another dozen yards, Nate was conscious that a subtle change had taken place. The mist was darker, the air a bit more chill. The thud of their hooves rang hollowly, as they would if walls hemmed them in. Soon he realized his hunch was right. He glimpsed stone surfaces on either side, and when he craned his neck, portions of a low ceiling were visible.

They were passing through a tunnel! Nate was elated beyond measure when he saw the mist begin to thin. Presently he could see the Anasazi. And that was not all. The end of the tunnel was a hundred yards distant, the pale glow that framed it serving as a beacon.

Pahchatka glanced at them, smiled, and rattled on in his birdsong tongue.

Nate checked behind his family. The wolf pack—if that was indeed what it had been—had not entered the tunnel. Once he learned to communicate better with their newfound friend, he would find out why.

"Pa, do you smell water?" Zach asked. His sense of smell had always been above average. Uncle Shakespeare was so impressed that he had the habit of calling Zach the Human Bloodhound.

Nate sniffed but registered only the same dank scent. Since they were nearing their goal and he was not hankering to antagonize the Anasazi, he said, "Remember. All of us must be on our best behavior once we reach the village. Don't say or do anything that would give them cause to lift our scalps."

"It's not what we'll do that worries me," Zach mentioned. "It's whether Pahchatka's people will be as friendly as he is."

"He'll vouch for us," Nate said confidently. He flattered himself that he was a fair judge of character, and the warrior impressed him as being a man of integrity.

"They might refuse to turn over the Ute boy," Winona said. "What then?"

"We're not leaving without Nevava."

The tunnel broadened, the ceiling rose. Nate removed the rope from around Evelyn's waist, coiled it, and placed it in the parfleche. By then they were thirty feet from the entrance, which was wide enough to permit two horses to walk side by side.

Pahchatka could no longer contain his excitement and ran on ahead. The Kings lost sight of him but heard his voice and those of others.

"If we have to," Nate said, "we'll trade for the boy. Offer them a knife and a couple of blankets." Little else could be spared. They had packed light for their journey, just the bare essentials; they would live off the land as they went.

The voice of Pahchatka climbed to an angry shout, then, in the bat of an eye, the warrior stopped talking. Someone else spoke harshly.

Nate gestured for his family to stop, and drew rein. "Hold it while I see what's going on," he said quietly. He slid off his horse and crept to the opening. Dense vegetation cloaked a narrow trail and prevented him from seeing what lay beyond. Cautiously, he stepped into the open, and as he leveled his rifle he remembered to his dismay that he had forgotten to reload it after firing at the thing in the mist. He had broken his mentor's first law of survival.

Above him, leaves shook. Nate looked up and saw two husky warriors balanced on a stout limb.

They had just dropped a net.

Chapter Six

Nate King tried to throw himself into the clear, but the cord web closed around him, entangling his arms and legs. He was brought crashing down. Heaving onto his knees, he frantically tried to break free. It was useless. The net had been ingeniously designed. The harder he struggled, the tighter the coils constricted. In moments he was wrapped as snug as a caterpillar in a cocoon.

The two Indians dropped lightly from the limb. From out of the undergrowth came four more, one of them Pahchatka. He looked glumly at Nate, his demeanor showing he did not approve of what had been done.

A tall warrior whose nose had once been broken and never mended properly walked to the net. Sneering at the mountain man, he drew back a foot to kick him, but at a protest from Pahchatka he desisted.

"Husband! Is anything wrong?"

At Winona's yell, the warriors melted into the vegetation. The pair who had tossed the net dragged Nate under cover with them. Nate opened his mouth wide to shout a warning, but one of the men clamped a hand over his mouth, stifling his outcry.

Inside the tunnel, Winona King grew uneasy. The commotion she had heard did not bode well. "Your father should have answered," she said softly.

"Want me to have a look-see?" Zach volunteered. He was more concerned about missing out on any excitement than he was worried for his pa's safety. His father had proven time and again that he could handle anything that came along, and Zach had unbounded confidence in him.

"No. We stick together," Winona said, hiding the anxiety that welled up within her. As her man would say, they were caught between a rock and a hard place. Her first instinct was to rush to his aid, but she did not know what was out there and refused to expose her children to further peril. Nor could they retrace their steps and try to find another way into the Anasazi sanctuary, not with those terrible wolflike beasts waiting in the mist.

Evelyn squirmed in her saddle. "What are we going to do, Ma?" She was all for riding on out and verifying that her father was all right.

"Nothing, for the moment." Winona dismounted and moved to the left-hand wall. They were safe enough where they were, since no one could get at them from either direction without being spotted.

"You can't be serious," Zach objected. "We can't desert Pa if he's in trouble."

"How dare you!" Winona gave in to a rare burst of anger. "When you have loved someone as I do your father, then you can criticize me. I would never desert him. When his time comes to die, I intend to be at his side and share his fate." Controlling her emotions, she said more calmly, "But it would not do for us to rush out. If something has happened, we are the only hope he has."

"I see your point," Zach said, yet he did not whole-heartedly agree with it. He would rather rush to the rescue with their guns blazing.

In the verdant growth that crowded the entrance, Nate King tried to bite the hand covering his mouth and could not. Thick strands of rope intervened. He was encouraged that his family had not fallen for the Anasazis' ruse. But his elation was short-lived.

The warrior with the crooked nose and two others slunk toward the tunnel. All three were dressed much like Pahchatka, and like him they were armed with curved war clubs. Crooked Nose flattened against the rock outcropping, then edged toward the opening.

Nate redoubled his efforts to warn his loved ones. He had almost succeeded in slipping his mouth free when a heavy blow to the back of his head exploded stars in front of his eyes and he sagged, dazed.

Inside the dark tunnel, Winona King glanced at her children. "Climb down and stay close to the walls," she directed. One thing was in their favor. They would be hard to spot from outside, but they had a clear shot at anyone who might try to enter.

Zach hopped down, then helped his sister off her pony. As he straightened, a face poked into sight, along with part of a war club. His mother was looking at them, not at the entrance, and she did not see the man's cruel features and oddly twisted countenance. Zach reacted without deliberation. Whirling, he aimed his rifle, cocking the hammer as he turned. Thunder pounded his ears when he stroked the trigger.

Outside, Nate saw Crooked Nose jerk back as rock slivers went flying. One raked the warrior's right cheek, digging a furrow and drawing blood.

The Anasazis huddled to confer, except for the one at the mountain man's side.

Pahchatka, Nate noticed, was totally ignored. His family's lone ally, the man Nate had counted on to establish peaceful relations with the tribe, apparently had no say in what the Anasazis did. Presently a warrior broke from the rest to jog off along a narrow trail. Crooked Nose and the others took up positions near the tunnel, and everyone settled down to wait.

Nate glanced at his guard. The man was coiled to bash him with the war club again if he acted up. For the moment his family was safe, so he lay still, testing the net for weak spots on the sly. There were none.

Outwardly, Nate put on a composed front. Inwardly, he churned with apprehension and overwhelming guilt. Should anything happen to Winona and the kids, it would be his fault. He was the one who had insisted on saving the Ute boy against impossible odds.

The minutes crawled by. The pale light grew brighter, but Nate could not yet see the sun over the mesa rim that reared above them. He wondered how his wife was faring, and dreaded her being harmed when the Anasazis made their move.

Winona was likewise thinking of him. She had posted Zach at the right-hand wall and made it plain he was not to shoot again unless she said to, or if their lives were in immediate danger. For all she knew, the warrior who had peeked inside had only wanted to palaver.

Evelyn was hunkered at her mother's knees. She was hungry and tired and scared to death, and she would rather be back in their cabin than anywhere else. It seemed to her that every time they went somewhere, something bad happened. They would be smart to stay home from then on and spare themselves the grief.

Off the top of her head, Evelyn commented, "When I get big, I'm going to live with the Shoshones the year round."

What brought that on? Winona mused. Aloud, she said, "That would be nice. I will come to visit you as often as I can. After you have children of your own, I will stay in your lodge for as long as you need me to help out.''

"I'm not having children, Ma.''

"You think so?''

"I know so. Sorry, but I'm never getting married. Boys are too icky. All they do is tease me and pull my hair. The only nice one is Pa, and he's taken.''

Winona laughed, despite their plight. Why was it almost all little girls and boys felt the same way? She had shared their outlook once. How old had she been? Seven? Eight? On several occasions she had seen older boys and girls sneak caresses, and her sensibilities had been shocked. Once she had accidentally caught an older friend kissing a young warrior. It had nearly made her sick. All that night she had tossed and turned, having nightmares about a boy's mouth touching hers. How silly she had—

The tramp of feet alerted Winona to a new development. Voices murmured, many more than before. She wondered what it meant.

Nate could have told her. Fifteen more warriors had arrived, led by a tall Anasazi in an elaborate outfit. Fringed white moccasins covered his feet. His legs had been painted black as high as his knees, which were adorned with red tassels of some kind. Instead of pants or a breechcloth, he wore what Nate could only describe as a white skirt sprinkled with painted symbols. His shirt was blue and brown. A wide necklace hung from his neck, while on his head rested a high headdress not at all like those worn on special occasions by the Shoshones and the Crows. It was circular, the feathers rising straight up.

The newcomer had great authority. At a gesture, Nate was dragged from the brush. The man examined him with probing dark eyes. Pahchatka spoke up, but Nate could not tell if the newcomer paid any attention.

Crooked Nose brought over Nate's Hawken, which had dropped to the ground when the net snared him. The newcomer inspected it with much interest. As for Nate's pistols, they were still under his belt, but he could not get at them. Nor could he unlimber his Green River knife.

Pahchatka stepped between Crooked Nose and the leader, who listened as Pahchatka talked on and on, frequently pointing at Nate and at the tunnel. Relating what had happened, Nate figured. He watched the leader's face closely and saw no hint of friendliness. His last hope had been dashed.

The chief turned to Crooked Nose. Instructions were given. Half the warriors filed to the right side of the entrance, half to the left. Their intent was transparent. They were going to charge in and overwhelm Winona and the children.

Nate glanced around. For the moment the Anasazis had forgotten about him. Even the guard was riveted to the scene about to unfold. Sucking in a breath, he hollered at the top of his lungs, "Look out! They're getting set to rush you!" He was going to say more, but the war club descended and the grass leaped up to meet his face.

Winona King's heart soared to learn her man was still alive. His warning galvanized her into spinning, grabbing Blue Flower, and practically throwing her daughter onto the pony. "Climb on your bay," she told Zach.

"What are you fixing to do?"

Winona had been thinking while they waited. She remembered how scared Pahchatka had been of their horses. It stood to reason that the rest of the tribe shared his outlook, and she aimed to exploit their fear. Slipping a foot into the mare's stirrup, she pulled herself up and grasped the reins. "When I give the word, you are to ride as if a grizzly is trying to catch us. Don't stop for anything or anyone. I will be right behind you."

59

"I should go last to cover the two of you," Zach said.

"No. I need you to lead your father's horse while I protect Blue Flower. We are counting on you, son, to fight your way through and clear a path for us."

Zach squared his shoulders. "Don't worry, Ma. I won't let you down."

Winona nudged her mare close to the pony. The Anasazis were bound to be so shocked when the first rider appeared that they would scatter like leaves in a gale. Stalking Coyote and Blue Flower would have the best chance to escape. As for herself, well, she had meant what she said about sharing her husband's fate if need be.

Outside, Nate King forced his sluggish mind to function and raised his head. The man with the headdress lifted an arm to signal the attack.

"Now!" Winona shouted, and as her son goaded the bay into a gallop and hauled on the stallion's reins, she smacked her daughter's pony on the flank with all her might. Lashing the mare into step behind them, she vented a Shoshone war whoop.

Zach King was tingling with the thrill of it all. Shrieking lustily, he reached the opening just as Anasazi warriors filled it. Their amazement was almost comical. The bay slammed into them like a living battering ram, bowling some over, scattering others right and left. He saw his father lying to one side, wrapped in a net, but he could not stop, not when his mother and sister were depending on him to get them to safety.

Evelyn was petrified. She clung to her pony with rigid fingers, scarcely breathing as she flew past stunned warriors. One recovered his wits and lunged at her.

Winona was right there. With a sweep of her rifle, the man was knocked sprawling into several of his companions. Then she was in the clear. She glimpsed her husband, helpless and under guard. For a fleeting instant their eyes locked, and it was as if a dam had broken deep within her, pouring all the love she bore him from her soul. *We will save you!* she mentally vowed.

Yells of outrage rose from the Anasazis. In a pack they sped in pursuit. Nate swung his legs into their path, tripping two. For his cleverness he was grabbed and punched and rolled a few yards away so he could not interfere.

The man in the headdress stood over him, glaring. Nate glared back. A pair of hefty warriors flanked the chief, and if looks could kill, they would have seared him to a cinder. Any likelihood of smoking the pipe of peace with the Anasazis was growing slimmer by the second.

Pahchatka was aloof, over beside a tree. His expression was an open book, revealing his disgust and resentment. He glanced at Nate as if to say, "I am sorry."

The drum of hooves faded fast. Nate listened for telltale outcries that might be a clue that his family had been captured. Fiery shouts blended with the crash of limbs. A horse whinnied stridently, and he feared that it had been brought down.

The chief addressed the guards. One hurried into the woods and returned bearing a long, relatively straight limb. Its purpose became apparent when Nate's wrists and ankles were tied to it. Each of the guards took an end.

Trussed like a deer, enmeshed in the net, Nate could only fume as he was borne along the trail at a brisk clip. In the lead was the chief. Pahchatka hung back, as glum as a rainy day.

The trail wound lower through verdant forest. To call it woodland did not do it justice. "Jungle" was more appropriate. Vines dangled in lush profusion, colorful flowers adorned the lower and middle terraces, gaily plumed birds warbled and chirped and cawed. Butterflies twice the size of those Nate was accustomed to flitted in thick clusters. The sweet scent Nate had caught wind of

61

now and then in the tunnel was thick enough to cut with a knife.

In due course the growth thinned. The chieftain stopped on the lip of a grassy terrace, affording Nate an unobstructed view of the Anasazis' domain. And what a domain it was!

The interior of the mesa was actually an oval valley approximately two miles in length and a mile wide. Towering cliffs encircled it, forming an impassable protective barrier, impassable except for the tunnel that came in under the bottom of the east wall. In the center a tranquil lake was home to ducks, brants, and geese. Goats and sheep grazed along the shore.

In a nearby meadow deer were feeding, deer much taller and broader than those that called the Rockies home, the bucks sporting antlers a moose would envy.

Nate forgot about the rope chafing his wrists and the numbness in his hips and legs. The incredible scene dazzled him. It was a literal paradise, a safe haven where the outside world did not intrude. Small wonder not many had ever heard of the People of the Mist.

A score of questions begged answers. How long had the Anasazis lived there? Where did they come from originally? Why had they set themselves apart from all the other tribes? Were the many unusual varieties of wildlife in the lost valley there before they came?

The leader adjusted his headdress, then started down the slope. A low cry from one of the men carrying Nate drew their attention to a spot on the cliff high to the north, and the Anasazis commenced chattering like agitated chipmunks.

Nate had to twist his neck to see. He caught a tantalizing sight of *something* as it skittered up the sheer surface, something enormous, something that vanished into the inky mouth of what could only be a cave. One of more than a dozen.

The Lost Valley

The Anasazis were visibly shaken, including Pah-chatka. Just as in the Garden of Eden, their paradise had a serpent in its midst. Or rather, a reptilian relative. For the creature Nate had seen was more like a lizard than a snake, a gigantic lizard with a blunt head, four legs, and a tail three times as long as its body.

The kachina.

Chapter Seven

Winona King flew down the narrow trail in her daughter's wake, ducking low limbs and dodging branches that spiked at them from either side. The howls of the Anasazis swelled in frustration. She glanced back and saw several of the fleetest doggedly sticking to the chase. One man, in particular, was as swift as an antelope, and almost came within throwing range of his war club.

But no human could ever match a horse. The warrior faltered, his steps flagging, his body caked with sweat. He shook a fist at them and shouted in impotent fury.

Winona smiled at him, which made him shake his fist more violently. Her plan had worked, but only because none of the Anasazis were armed with bows and arrows.

Another low limb materialized directly ahead. Winona bent over the saddle, her chest rubbing against the mare's mane. The limb whisked overhead. She saw Blue Flower look back, so she waved.

Evelyn was close to tears. The more she thought about

leaving her father in the clutches of those bad men, the more upset she became. They might kill him. Until that moment, she had never really imagined that her pa could die. She had always regarded him as the bravest, strongest, smartest man alive. She had always pictured him as invincible. But seeing him in that net, seeing him so helpless, unable to lift a finger to protect himself, made her realize that he was flesh and blood like everyone else.

A cackle made Evelyn look up. Her brother was laughing and shaking his rifle at her. She rode sadly on, unable to see what he was so happy about.

Zach was thrilled by their escape. The heady excitement had his blood racing, his temples pounding. It was moments like these, he reflected, that all true warriors lived for! The next time his family visited his mother's people, he would have a fine tale to tell the other boys.

A sharp bend reminded Zach to concentrate on the matter at hand. He galloped along until an open hilltop appeared. Rather than expose himself, he brought the stallion to a halt and moved to one side. Within seconds his sister and mother had joined him. "What now, Ma?" he asked.

Winona disliked putting more distance between them and her husband, but the Anasazis were bound to try to track them down. Saving Nate would have to wait until after they eluded the trackers. She had her pick of going north or south. On a whim, she spurred the mare northward. "Follow me."

Zach reluctantly obeyed. He would rather wait in hiding and drop the first few Anasazis who showed up, then light a shuck for heavy timber. The screech of a bizarre bird awakened him to how strange their surroundings were. It had a red head, a yellow body, and tail feathers as long as his arm. He had never set eyes on a bird quite like it. Nor could he identify many of the trees and lesser plants.

Zach grew confused. His pa had made it a point to teach him about every wild animal and all the varieties of plant life found in the Rockies. It was essential. To survive, a man had to know all there was to know about everything he came across. He had to know which plants were edible, which were not. Which thrived near water. Which were good for burning. And so on.

The lore his father taught had been expanded on by some of the Shoshones. Certain ones, like the old healer lady, had stored an incredible amount of knowledge they were gladly willing to share.

Zach had assumed he knew all there was worth learning, but now he saw that he had been mistaken. So much here was new, so much was strikingly different. He saw a long, thin green snake with oversized eyes. He spotted a large hawk with feathers on its head that jutted out at an angle instead of lying flat. He saw a small animal that seemed to be a cross between a deer and an antelope. What was this place? he marveled.

Winona had been studying the lay of the land. The stone ramparts not only safeguarded the tribe from outside enemies, they trapped any outsiders caught inside. Even if she rescued Nate, eventually the Anasazi would hunt them down and slay them.

It did not help any that the soil was so fertile, so rich and soft. Their mounts left a trail a four-year-old could follow.

She passed a bush bearing round reddish berries, and her stomach growled. But she left the berries alone, since she had no way of telling if they were safe or poisonous. "Don't touch these," she told her children.

Evelyn was not hungry anyway. She was too sad to be hungry. All she could think of was her father and how very much she loved him.

Zach kept twisting to check their back trail. All he wanted was a clear shot at one of the Anasazis. Just one.

The Lost Valley

Time passed. Once the sun rose above the mesa's rim, the temperature soared. By the middle of the morning Winona was sweltering. She swatted at a large ugly insect with a thin needlelike nose that alighted on her arm. Farther on she tensed when a spider the size of her hand scuttled up a tree.

Winona decided she would not like to live in this valley. It had an air about it, a feeling of menace that had nothing to do with the unfriendly Anasazis. It was bad medicine. Her people had learned long ago to shun such spots. Certain lakes and streams and mountains were always avoided because they brought disaster down on the shoulders of anyone foolish enough to defy the taboo.

One lake came to mind. It was way up in the mountain range that the whites called the Tetons. Long ago, back when only Indians roamed the land, back when the Shoshones were new to the earth, her people had camped at that lake. The next morning a Shoshone maiden and her suitor had gone rowing in a canoe. Watchers on shore had been horrified when an enormous creature heaved out of the water, shattering the canoe, and took the maiden into its huge jaws. The suitor had pulled his knife and tried to save her, but the doomed girl was pulled under the surface and never seen again.

A water horse, her people called it. One of many in different lakes. Lakes that were bad medicine. Just like the valley.

Presently, Winona noticed that the vegetation was thinning, the ground becoming rockier. They were near the north wall of the escarpment. Midway up were a number of dark openings she judged to be the mouth of caves.

The mare started to act skittish. Every so often it would toss its head and snort for no reason at all.

Winona came to the end of the trees and grinned. A wide belt of solid rock rimmed the base of the cliff, extending for as far as she could see in either direction.

Their horses would leave no tracks on it. "Let the An-asazis try to follow us now," she said, riding out of the shade into the glaring heat. She crossed to the cliff and reined up. "We'll rest here a spell."

Above them were the caves. Up close, the cliff face was pockmarked with holes and cracks and fissures. Winona noted a lot of deep scratch marks she could not account for. Dismounting, she unslung the water skin and opened it. "Anyone thirsty besides me?"

Evelyn drank first. As her mother tilted the water skin, she bent her head partway back. Her gaze drifted to the dark openings high overhead. For a fraction of an instant she thought that she saw something jut out from one of the lowest caves, something big. But then she blinked and it was gone.

Convinced it could not have been real, Evelyn drank with relish. She told herself that she should be glad, not sad. After all, they were safe for the moment, weren't they?

A well-worn series of footpaths led from the terraces toward the lake. Nate King swayed with every stride the warriors took, his wrists and ankles lanced by aching pangs. He was so depressed by the turn of events that he did not take much interest in the landscape until they had descended three levels.

The grassy slopes were not as smooth as they should have been. The grass grew in grooved sections, grooves that Nate recognized for what they had once been: neatly arranged furrows, such as a plow might make. Once, not all that long ago, the terraces had been tilled.

Lower down, Nate's guess was confirmed. The tiers closest to the lake were being worked by near-naked Anasazi farmers, men and women alike, tending crops of corn, squash, pumpkins, and other vegetables. They had a variety of implements: hoes, rakes, short sickles, and more. Most stopped what they were doing to stare.

As yet Nate had not seen the Anasazi village. He scoured the shore and a small plain beyond for their lodges, which he assumed would be made of wood since the Anasazis lived too far from the plains to rely on a steady supply of buffalo hides for tepees.

Then he looked to the south, where a section of the cliff had long ago collapsed and was piled high in deep shadow. As his captors stepped from the last terrace onto a wide dirt avenue, the rubble began to take on definite form, to acquire a symmetrical shape. It was not rubble at all, but an immense city situated at the base of the rampart.

Nate was dumbfounded. As his captors neared their destination, the sun cleared the mesa, bathing the entire valley in a golden glow. The Anasazi city was revealed in all its majestic glory.

It was an architectural wonder, a gigantic structure that resembled a horseshoe in its outline. Hundreds of rooms were stacked one on top of another in ever-higher layers or rings. The innermost was a single story high, the outermost three or four stories. The open end of the horseshoe faced the lake.

The only thing Nate could compare it to was a tremendous honeycomb. People were bustling about on the roofs, which were linked by ladders. A central stairway led from the plaza to the roof of the dwellings that abutted the cliff.

Nate was so entranced by the city that he almost didn't notice a curious aspect to the lake. A broad belt of dried mud ringed it, evidence that the lake was shrinking. He judged it to be only a third the size it once had been. Whether the shrinkage was seasonal, a result of the hot weather, or caused by some other agency, he could not say.

They passed Anasazis going about their daily routines.

Farmers trudging to or from the terraces, hunters heading to or coming from the jungle, warriors on official business. A party of the latter were stopped by the man in the headdress, and at a command from him, they fell into step to the rear, two of them replacing the pair who had carried Nate so far.

One of the warriors was sent ahead at a sprint. When he was within earshot of the city, he began hollering.

The town crier, Nate observed. People moved toward the plaza. Some on the roofs stepped to the edges so they could see better. From a large building set apart from the honeycomb came half a dozen men in stately feathered garb.

Nate's wrists had grown numb. He rubbed them back and forth to restore circulation and felt a wet, sticky sensation trickle toward his left elbow. The skin had broken, and he was bleeding. But it was nothing compared to the agony in his shoulders and the pain in his parched throat. The glistening lake, so near yet so unattainable, only aggravated his thirst.

A sizable crowd had gathered by the time Nate's captors reached the plaza. In the forefront stood the group in feathered outfits. The man in the headdress stopped in front of them and greeted them solemnly.

"Put me down, damn you," Nate groused when it became obvious his bearers were not going to do so.

A tall Anasazi bedecked in yellow and red feathers strode over. He wore an outlandish mask crafted to mimic a bird's head. From between the open beak dark eyes bored into Nate's. A guttural voice rang out.

Crooked Nose appeared at the bird-man's side. They talked at length, and when they were done it was Pahchatka's turn to be quizzed. Hope bloomed in the depths of Nate's being, hope that withered like a blossom in the desert as Pahchatka became more impassioned and the bird-man—or High Chief, as Nate had taken to thinking of him—grew ever more stern. It did not bode well.

Finally Pahchatka bowed his head and walked away, the look he cast at Nate conveying a world of meaning.

At a command from the High Chief, Nate was unceremoniously dumped on the ground. Caught off guard, he grunted and winced as pain shot up his left arm and along his ribs. Fingers pried at the net, loosening it, and before long the Anasazis had unwrapped it and cut the bonds that held his limbs fast to the pole. He was free, but his legs were so deadened that he could not stand on his own. He tried after being kicked several times and prodded by a warrior's club.

The High Chief spoke, and two men seized hold of the mountain man. Roughly jerking him erect, they moved toward the east end of the horseshoe. Three warriors took up positions on either side.

Talking excitedly, the crowd parted to let them pass. Nate saw scores of swarthy faces, but not one he would rate as friendly until he was almost through them. That was when he spotted a face that did not belong, a face that was Mexican, not Anasazi. There could be no doubt, even though the man was dressed in typical Anasazi attire. A prisoner? Nate wondered, and smiled, only to feel his insides turn to ice when he saw that the man was blind. Scarred pits existed where the eyelids should be. *"Hola, amigo!"* he croaked, but received no reply.

The warriors dragged him to a ladder. One shoved him so that he fell against it, and if Nate's arms and legs had not been so stiff that he could barely move, he would have punched the man full in the mouth. "Hold your horses, damn you!" he complained. It was a waste of breath. A war club jabbed him in the ribs, inciting him further.

"I hope the kachina eats every one of you," Nate fumed, with astounding results. The nearest warriors stepped back, and all of them fingered their weapons.

What had he done? Why were they giving him a wide berth? "Is it the kachina?" he said aloud, and was rewarded by having one of the warriors weave a symbol in the air and intone a few words as if to ward off an evil spirit.

Nate laughed bitterly. The Anasazis feared the thing that had slain the Utes. They even feared its name. Or was there something more to it? Whatever the case, he could not resist licking his lips and yelling just as loudly as he could, "Kachina! Kachina! Kachina!"

Every last Anasazi froze. Mothers clutched children. Men muttered, many gazing at the cliffs above their city with what could only be described as barely concealed fear.

No one molested Nate as he slowly scaled the ladder to a flat roof. Six of the warriors followed him, and the one who had pushed him walked to a hole in the center and motioned at the top of a ladder that jutted from the square opening.

"You want me to go down there?" Nate deduced. His legs were working well enough for him to manage it nicely. The interior was musty but cool, refreshingly so. At the bottom he straightened and waited for his eyes to adjust to the murk. He shifted, and as soon as he turned his back to the ladder, it was yanked up.

Nate glanced at the opening, the *only* opening, apparently. The warrior who had pushed him was smirking. And why not? The Anasazis had him right where they wanted him; they could do with him as they pleased.

They could even kill him.

Chapter Eight

The stallion started acting up only a few minutes after Winona had called the halt. She was seated, her back to the cliff, when the big black snorted and pawed the ground, then looked up, way up, bending its neck as far as a horse could.

"What's the matter with him, Ma?" Blue Flower asked. She was so hot she couldn't stand it. The drink from the water skin had barely slaked her thirst.

"I don't know," Winona answered, and glanced up. From that angle it was like gazing over an endless pockmarked expanse of stone dotted by black patches. The cave mouths yawned wide. They would have been an ideal haven for her and the children if they were not so high up.

Zach was pacing and watching the woodland. As yet there had been no sign of the Anasazis, but that was bound to change. He took the responsibility of protecting his mother and sister with the utmost seriousness. If his pa had told him once, his pa had told him a hundred times that it would be up to him to look after them if the unthinkable happened.

Winona pushed her hair back and leaned her head against the cliff. She closed her eyes to savor a few moments of rest. But she was too agitated to relax. Nate needed her. She must think of a means of saving him, and the Ute boy, as well.

Something brushed her face. Thinking it was a fly or some other insect, Winona idly swatted the air without opening her eyes. Again it brushed her, this time on her forehead. She swung both hands, listening for the buzz of tiny wings. Hearing none, she sighed and sat up and gazed around. Whatever had landed on her was gone.

Winona was pleased at how well her children were holding up. Stalking Coyote had fought enemies before and had exhibited a degree of courage that might one day result in a position of leadership among the Shoshones. Blue Flower, though, had lived a generally sheltered, safe existence. As would most any mother, Winona had done all she could to protect her daughter from the worst life had to offer. Sometimes, Winona would scold herself for being too protective. But how else should she act? Motherly instinct was deeply ingrained. A woman could no more resist it than she could resist basic urges like hunger and the nightly need for sleep.

Once more something lightly touched Winona, this time on the chin. She saw no insect, nothing to account for it. Suddenly a tiny piece of stone fell into her lap with a *plop*. Mystified, she twisted and craned her neck. Specks of dust and motes of dirt were fluttering toward her from on high. She moved away from the wall and stood, an instant before a rock the size of a walnut hit in the exact spot she had been.

The particles were falling from the mouth of the lowest cave. The only explanation Winona could think of was that something was moving about up there and had dislodged debris on the cave floor. A silly notion, since the only creatures able to reach the caves were birds and she had not seen a single one fly anywhere near them.

A feeling came over her, a gut-wrenching feeling that she and the children were in great peril. She tried to tell herself that it was a wild fancy, that her nerves were frayed and her mind was not behaving logically, but the premonition persisted, growing stronger by the moment.

"We're leaving," Winona announced.

"So soon?" Evelyn said. She wouldn't have minded another swig from the water skin and maybe a short nap.

"Now."

Zach mounted without objecting. To stay in the open invited disaster. They needed to find cover and come up with a plan to save his father. Without being bidden, he grasped the stallion's reins.

Winona gave Blue Flower a boost into the saddle. After mounting the mare, she led them along the cliff's base, circling the valley in the direction of a lake that sparkled like a giant jewel.

She was puzzled by the absence of the Anasazis. Swift trackers would have been there by then. Either the warriors were taking their sweet time, or they had given up the chase, which was preposterous.

Or was it? Winona put herself in the Anasazis' moccasins and saw the situation in a whole new light. Why should the warriors wear themselves out chasing quarry on horseback? All the Anasazis had to do was post a sufficient number of men at the tunnel, and Winona and the kids were as good as caught.

They couldn't get out of the valley. They would have to live constantly on the run, never having a moment of real peace, always on the lookout for the Anasazis. It would wear them down, weaken them. Sooner or later they were bound to blunder and the Anasazis would snare them.

Winona resolved then and there that it was not going to happen that way. She would think of something. She had to.

The clatter of hooves on stone was uncomfortably loud. Winona veered to the tree line, where the soft clomp would not carry as far on the wind.

The presence of the breeze was a minor puzzle in itself. Winona would have thought that the towering ramparts would block the wind. Did it come over the top? Through the caves? Or were there other openings she did not know about, openings that might offer a safe route from the valley?

It was midday when the lush vegetation ended on the crest of a grassy terrace. Reining up, Winona crawled to the edge and peeked over. Slope after grassy slope rippled down to the valley floor. In the distance, near the lake, figures moved about. She could not quite make out what they were doing.

A bright shaft of reflected sunlight to the south pinpointed the Anasazi village. But what a village! Enormous beyond belief, it shone in the sunshine. She knew that was where her husband had been taken, so that was where she must go. But how to get there without getting caught?

Winona started to stand when the ground under her feet moved. The horses whinnied, Blue Flower cried out, and Winona flung her arms down to keep from falling. A muffled rumbling filled the valley. Trees swayed, the cliffs to the west seemed to shake violently, and the very air vibrated. The birds in the forest squawked shrilly, and somewhere in the brush a small animal bleated.

The effect did not last long. Within seconds the ground stilled, the rumbling died. Winona pushed upright and surveyed the valley. All appeared normal.

The Lost Valley

"What was that, Ma?" Evelyn asked. She had never heard of the whole earth quaking like that, and she cast wide eyes at the crags above, terrified that they would topple, crashing down on top of her.

Zach answered first. "I know what it was. An earthquake. Pa told me about them, how one shook him when he was a little boy. They're nothing to be scared of."

Winona did not share her son's outlook. Quakes were infrequent in the region the Shoshones roamed, but they did happen on occasion. Once, many winters past, so the story went, a quake had opened a wide crack that swallowed several warriors whole and then closed again, burying them alive.

"We must find a place to rest until sunset," Winona said, stepping to the mare. As she lifted her leg, a bellow rose from the nearby undergrowth.

Into the open bounded Anazasi warriors.

Nate King was lying on his side when the quake struck. He had made repeated circuits of the room, confirming that the only entrance was the hole in the roof. Grooves in one of the walls hinted that at one time a door to another apartment had existed but been walled over.

The construction fascinated him. The walls were made of stone embedded in mud mortar. Wooden beams braced the ceiling. The craftsmanship was outstanding. Overall, it rivaled a typical New York home.

His estimation of the Anasazis jumped considerably. In all his wide-flung travels, in all his contacts with Indians from the Mississippi to the Pacific, from Canada to the Texas border, he had never met a tribe quite like them. No one else, absolutely no one, built buildings on the scale of the Anasazis. Their city was an engineering masterpiece, as different from the hide tepees and brush wigwams of other tribes as night was from day.

The scope of their expertise was food for thought. Where had they learned such advanced techniques? How was it that none of the other tribes ever duplicated their achievements? What set the Anasazis apart from everyone else?

In a corner Nate found additional proof of their extraordinary talent. Someone had left behind a number of pots and baskets so exquisitely made that Nate could have sold them for many dollars to art collectors in New York City.

One prime example was a wickerwork vessel in the shape of a long cylinder. Bits of turquoise and small shells had been inlaid on the outer surface. It was flawless.

Another work of art was a black-and-red basket. Nate carried it under the rooftop opening so he could study its intricate design. The patterns had been woven from thick fibers with a precision that bespoke a master craftsman or craftswoman.

Nate also found a large striped sack that had seen better days. It was worn and torn but it was softer to lie on than the floor, so he spread it out and lay down. Sparkling shafts of sunlight streaming in through the hole lit up the center of the room but could not brighten the corners. He folded his arms and was mulling his bleak prospects when the whole apartment shimmied and shook.

In a flash Nate was on his feet. He had not experienced an earthquake since he was eight. His father had taken him to an uncle's farm for a week, and while there a rare quake had rattled upper New York. It had not done any damage or killed anyone, but to his young mind it had been a revelation. The planet had fits, just as people did.

Now Nate moved to the middle of the floor in case the ceiling collapsed or the walls buckled. The shaking stopped, and he breathed easier. Outside, the buzz of Anasazi voices had risen in alarm.

The Lost Valley

A shadow fell across the opening. The head and shoulders of a man were silhouetted against the azure sky as he dipped onto his knees and poked his head below the rim. *"Hola, señor. Esta conversacion es sin ambages ni rodeos, asi que escucha astentamente."*

Nate recognized the blind Mexican from the plaza. "I'm sorry, but I don't speak Spanish all that well. Do you savvy English?"

"Sí, señor," the man said. "I speak it some." He lowered an arm. "Can you reach my hand?"

"It's too high."

"I was afraid of that." The man elevated his head to listen. "Pay attention. I do not have much time. When the ground shakes, the Anasazis are scared. But they do not stay scared long. My name is Pedro Valdez, and I am from Sonora."

"What are you doing here?" Nate asked. Sonora was a northern Mexican province hundreds of miles to the south. "You're a long way from home."

The man's scarred eyelids moved as the eyes under them shifted toward the sound of Nate's voice. "How well I know it. Four years ago I was a vaquero on a hacienda. I made a good wage, and I had plans to marry a pretty senorita. One night, as I rode herd, I was captured by Indians."

"The Anasazis?" Nate broke in.

"No. Navajos. They traded me to the Anasazis." Pedro extended two fingers and touched his eyelids. "They saw to it I can never escape."

The full implication jarred Nate with the force of a physical blow. "They blinded you on purpose?"

"Sí. With the flat of a red-hot blade."

"My Lord."

"They will do the same to you. If they do not feed you to the kachinas."

The mention of the creature that had slaughtered the

79

Utes prompted Nate to ask, "What are those things? I tracked one from the mountains to this mesa and never really had a good look at it."

"The kachinas are spirits made flesh," Pedro said. "Or so the Anasazis believe. Me, I say they are demons." He paused. "They don't often stray from their caves. The one you followed killed two men and went out the tunnel. Warriors hunted it, but they could not catch it. So they say. I think they were afraid." Pedro raised his head. "I must go. Someone comes."

"Wait! One last thing. Do you know of an Ute boy named Nevava?"

"Tokipha brought a new boy, I am told."

"I aim to get him out of here. You, too, if you want to go along."

Pedro grew downcast. "I wish it were so simple. No one ever escapes the Anasazis. Many have tried. None have succeeded." Standing, he shook his head in sorrow. "I am most sorry, *señor*. One way or another, you will end your days here. Accept it and you will be better off."

"Never," Nate declared, but there was no one to hear. Pedro had vanished, moving with surprising speed for someone who was sightless. "Come back when you can!" Nate shouted, the cry echoing hollowly. In the Mexican's absence he felt keenly alone, pathetically vulnerable. The four walls seemed more confining, the room seemed gloomier, matching his spirits.

Nate walked in a circle under the opening, racking his brain for a miracle. Knowing it was useless, he backed up a dozen paces, coiled, then hurtled forward and upward. His spring swept him high in a vaulting arc—but nowhere near high enough. His outflung hand missed the rim by several feet.

Confined spaces had never bothered Nate, yet suddenly he could not stand being in that room. He wanted out. Unbridled panic clawed at his insides and he wildly roved the chamber, seeking salvation. There had to be a way. There just had to be.

He thought of his makeshift blanket, of the striped sack. Examining the weave, he found a loose end, which he pried at with a fingernail. It was painstaking work, but he slowly unraveled it and wound the heavy twine or whatever it was around his left hand. When he had enough for his purposes, he walked to the corner where the baskets and other items had been left. Broken pottery shards sufficed for the next step. Selecting the sharpest, he cut the twine.

There was nothing to use as a hook. He had to settle for the elaborate vessel decorated with turquoise. Wrapping the twine around the middle, he made a knot, then wrapped it from top to bottom and tied another.

It was crude, but it might work. Nate swung the vessel around and around, leaving little slack. At the apex of a swing he launched it at the opening. His insane scheme called for somehow snagging the ladder that must be lying near the entrance.

The vessel soared up and out, and he heard it thud onto the roof. Gingerly, Nate pulled, but it did not catch on anything and soon appeared at the lip. ''Consarn it.'' Nate moved under the opening and tugged. The vessel was supposed to fall into his hands, but it rose instead, the twine giving a hard jerk.

A leering face explained why. Crooked Nose held the vessel for Nate to see, then slashed the twine with a knife. He flipped the vessel, caught it, and strolled off, his mocking laughter boiling the mountain man's blood.

Nate had to face the truth. There was no way out.

No way out at all.

Chapter Nine

Winona King had split seconds in which to make up her mind what to do. Since charging the Anasazis had worked once, she thought it might work again. Consequently, as she sprang onto the mare, she reined the horse around. The turn saved her, for as the animal rotated, a war club flashed past, missing her head by inches.

Other warriors cocked their arms to throw. Zach had his rifle up and extended, and fired at the foremost. The ball cored the man's shoulder, crumpling him in his tracks.

"Down the hill!" Winona bawled. The shot scattered most of the Anasazis, who dived flat or sought cover. She saw Blue Flower flee over the crest and cut the reins to follow. From out of nowhere a bronzed hand streaked, grabbing the mare's bridle. A stocky warrior intended to take her alive.

Winona kicked, striking him in the chest. The Anasazi staggered but held on. Grimly, Winona drove the stock of her rifle at his head. Others were closing in, and if she did not break free quickly it would all be over. The man holding on to the mare lunged, his other hand seeking her leg.

"Ma!"

Zach barreled to his mother's side, wielding his Hawken as if it were a club. It smashed into the warrior's chin as the man shifted to confront him. A shove, and the warrior was prone, holding his broken jaw. "Ride, Ma! Ride!"

Winona did not waste another moment. She galloped on her daughter's heels and glanced back to make sure Stalking Coyote was following her. The air sizzled to war clubs deftly thrown, but only one connected, a glancing blow off her son's shoulder as the bay cleared the rim.

Zach had to grit his teeth to keep from crying out. Excruciating pain spiked through him, and his left arm went numb. Gamely, he sped on down the slope as the Anasazis spilled over it in his wake.

Evelyn slowed at the bottom of the first terrace. Below lay open ground, and her father had always told her to seek cover when bad men were after her. She looked at her mother for guidance, yelling, "Which way?"

Winona saw that the figures on the valley floor were not moving. They had heard the shot, and some might rush up to help the warriors. She and the children would be caught between the two groups, trapped with nowhere to run. To the north lay the rocky belt that bordered the ramparts. To the south the terraces stretched for half a mile, blending into thick forest.

"That way!" Winona said, jabbing southward.

For her age Evelyn was a superb rider. Her parents had placed her on a horse when she was barely old enough to walk, and by the time she was seven she could ride as well as most grown men. Now she proved it by wheeling her pony on the edge of a coin and making for the distant woodland at breakneck speed.

The Anasazis shrieked and yipped like bloodthirsty Blackfeet. They gave chase, but it was the same story as before. They soon fell behind, shrieking all the louder.

Some of the people below were working their way up. Winona was not worried; they couldn't possibly cut the horses off before the animals reached the trees. She should feel relieved, but she wasn't; she was only delaying the inevitable. The lost valley was simply too small for the three of them to elude the Anasazis forever.

She squinted skyward at the sun, which was on its descent but would not set for hours. Night offered the promise of temporary safety. Or did it? The huge tracks of the monster that slew Red Feather's hunting party had led into the valley, so the creature must be there, somewhere. If it was like most meat-eaters, it would be most active after the sun went down.

Why did the Anasazis stay, with a beast like that abroad in their midst? Winona's own people wanted nothing to do with the things that should not be, the creatures left over from the old time, creatures like the water horses, the hairy giants and the snakes that could swallow a horse whole.

The elders of her tribe said that in days long gone the creatures had been much more numerous and had constantly plagued the Shoshones and others.

She was thankful the twilight dwellers were now rare. The hairy giants had been driven from Shoshone territory before she was born. And no one had seen a giant snake in more moons than most could count, although a Crow claimed to have stumbled on one out on the prairie and barely escaped with his life.

The worst had been the red-haired cannibals. For many generations they had hunted people as others hunted game. The cannibals had even taken the dead for food.

The Lost Valley

This unspeakable state of affairs had gone on until the Paiutes waged bitter war against the cannibal tribe and wiped most of them out. Most, but not all. In remote regions of the mountains a few were said to linger on, devouring anyone unlucky enough to cross their path.

Then there were the NunumBi, or the little ones. They were dwarfs who lived in holes in the ground and went about armed with small but very powerful bows. Expert archers, they could pierce a man's eye at a hundred paces. In the old times the NunumBi had bitterly contested the spread of the red man, wreaking a great slaughter before they were themselves almost wiped out. Now they lurked in shadowy canyons and refuges deep in the mountains, and every so often a lone warrior would be found dead with tiny arrows jutting from his body.

Winona had never seen a red-haired cannibal, or a hairy giant or a NunumBi, but that did not mean they did not exist. She believed all the stories, heart and soul. Just as her parents had believed, and their parents before them.

Nate had laughed when she told him the tales. For a week after she imparted all she knew about the NunumBi, he had made a show of peering under tables and behind boulders to "make sure none of those uppity midgets are out to get us." When he learned of the cannibals, every now and then he would bite himself on the arm and say, "Not bad. A little salt and I'd taste downright delicious."

Men could be so irritating.

A yell from Zach brought an end to Winona's reverie. A lone warrior was scaling the terraces well ahead of the pack. The man was too far off to intercept them, but he held a bow, the first Winona had seen any of the Anasazis use.

Planting himself, the warrior whipped a shaft from a

quiver on his back, notched the arrow to the sinew string, and took deliberate aim.

Hope always sprang eternal. The saying was as old as the proverbial hills, yet as true as life.

Nate King did not give up—not even after Crooked Nose had ruined his attempt to snare the ladder. Nate had gone to the corner, rummaged among a pile of pottery shards until he found the biggest, and walked to the doorway that had been walled off. The mortar was newer, so perhaps, just perhaps, it would be easier to pick apart.

He gouged the sharp end of the shard into a likely spot and soon had a furrow dug. At the rate he was going, he estimated it would take him hours to make an opening large enough for him to crawl through. He kept at it, ignoring the tiny cuts and scrapes on his fingers and the pain in his wrist and knuckles.

So engrossed was Nate in his work that he did not realize he had company until a heavy footstep above snapped him erect. Flinging the shard down, he moved to the center of the room just as several heads appeared.

Crooked Nose was back, this time with friends. The ladder was lowered, and Crooked Nose beckoned.

Nate climbed out, blinking in the glare. Eight Anasazis ringed the opening, among them the High Chief in the bird outfit, the man in the tall headdress, and Pahchatka. Also present was Pedro, standing well back, his head bowed and his hands meekly folded. "What is this?" Nate asked the Mexican. "Are they here to put out my eyes?"

Pedro looked up, but he was clearly afraid to talk without permission. He shook his head once and bowed it again.

The High Chief barked, and Pedro stepped forward. Valdez listened closely as he was given instructions.

"I am to translate, *señor*. They have many questions

about you. You must always tell the truth or they will punish you.''

The threat carried no weight with Nate, not when the Anasazis had no way of knowing if he was lying or not. ''Tell them I will cooperate, but only if they agree to answer a few questions of my own.''

Licking his lips, Pedro placed a hand on Nate's sleeve. ''Please, my friend. Do not anger them. They do not like outsiders. Some need only a small excuse and they will torture you until you beg for them to end the misery.''

Nate could guess whom Pedro referred to. Crooked Nose was fondling his knife as if Nate were a turkey he could not wait to carve into. ''What do they have against outsiders?''

''Outsiders bring them death and sickness. Once, the Anasazis ruled this land. They had many cities. They were peaceful and happy.'' Pedro looked at the High Chief. When the man did not object, he continued. ''Then new tribes came. They waged war. Many Anasazis were killed, many cities destroyed.'' Pedro paused. ''One day a man came from the south. A Spaniard, from what they tell me. They had never seen anyone like him. They took him in, tried to nurse him. But he was too far gone. Soon many were sick. Hundreds died.''

Nate saw the Anasazis in a whole new light. It was a terrible tale, one that had been repeated recently. Not long ago there had been a friendly tribe on the upper Missouri, the Mandans. Nate had known many of them personally, and had been a guest of honor at the marriage of their leader's daughter to an Englishman.

Next to the Shoshones, the Mandans had been among the staunchest allies of the whites. Trappers were welcome in any of their villages. The Mandans gladly shared whatever they had. They traded pelts for trade goods, receiving guns, powder, blankets, and more. It was an arrangement that benefited both sides, until that awful day when the whites unwittingly gave the unsuspecting Mandans something that devastated them: smallpox.

"These are the last of the Anasazis," Pedro was saying. "This is their last city. Once they are gone, the tribe is gone."

"Tell them that if they let me go, I won't tell anyone on the outside about them. I'll keep the existence of their city a secret. They have nothing to worry about."

"It would do no good, *señor*. They will not let you leave. They are here now to see if they will kill you or keep you as a slave, like me."

The High Chief smacked Pedro's shoulder, then rambled on for over a minute. When he gestured, Pedro turned back. "Wakonhomin wants to know where you are from. They have never seen a white man before."

"Just tell him I come from the rising sun." Nate had an inspiration. "Also tell him that if they do not let me go, many more white men will come, and many of their warriors will be killed. Their war clubs are no match for our guns."

"You do not want me to say that."

"Tell him."

Nate waited as Valdez relayed his statements. Crooked Nose and most of the others scowled. Wakonhomin's bird mask shook as he wagged a short painted stick and curtly replied.

"He says you lie, *señor*. You would not have found this place if Pahchatka had not brought you. The mist and the red wolves keep the Anasazis safe."

The High Chief was no one's fool. Nate chose his next words much more carefully. "Ask him to be reasonable, Pedro. I'm only here for the Ute boy they took. I promised the boy's dying father I would take him back."

Pedro was going to say something, but Wakonhomin interrupted. "He says that your woman, that your *hijo* and *hija*, your son and your daughter, have not been caught. But they soon will be. If the kachinas do not get them first.''

Nate glanced toward the terraces and the jungle beyond. Dread for his family almost spurred him into making a desperate bid for freedom. He could leap from the low roof and hit the ground running. But he restrained himself. Scores of Anasazis were in the plaza, scores more tilling the lower terraces. He wouldn't get five hundred yards.

The High Chief had more to say, and Valdez dutifully translated. ''You are not sick like the Spaniard was. So they will not kill you right away.''

''Tell him thanks for nothing.''

Pedro did no such thing. ''He wants to strike a bargain with you, *señor*.''

''What kind of bargain?''

''They are most interested in your horses. They have seen horses before, ridden by Utes and others. But the Anasazis have never had any of their own.'' Wakonhomin talked awhile. ''He wants you to teach his people all you know about them: how to ride, how to breed many more. It will make their tribe strong. And if they must leave here, they can take more belongings with them.''

''Why would they abandon the last of their cities?''

''This place was a garden when first they came. But now there is much bad medicine. The ground shakes often. The lake is drying up. The kachinas grow bolder. And their women are not having as many babies as they once did.''

Now that Pedro mentioned it, Nate realized there were far fewer inhabitants than there should be. A city that size could accommodate more than a thousand without crowding. Yet he had seen only a few hundred. The Anasazis were in jeopardy of becoming extinct, like the Mandans. ''What do I get if I agree to teach them?''

"They will spare your life, and the lives of your *familia*."

"Will they let us go eventually?"

Pedro posed the question. It sparked a heated argument between the High Chief and Pahchatka. While they squabbled, Pedro sidled next to Nate. "If you do make it out, *señor*, I would be in your debt if you would send a letter to Mr. Jonathan Levi in San Antonio, Texas. Have him give my love to my *padre* and *madre*." As an afterthought, Pedro added, "I spent six years on his ranch. It is where I learned English."

"If I make it out, you're coming along," Nate reiterated.

"I would only slow you down." Pedro raised his scarred eyes to the heavens. "Once, I prayed to go home. Now I do not want to. Look at me. What could I do for a living? Be a beggar? Sit on a street corner and plead for pesos? I would rather die."

The argument ended and the High Chief cleared his throat. "Wakonhomin says that you must give up thoughts of leaving. You will spend the rest of your days with his people. So will your family. And if any of you try to escape, all of you will have done to your eyes what was done to mine." Pedro paused. "I am sorry."

So was Nate. The Anasazis were leaving him no choice. With a little outside help the tribe might survive the current crisis. But if they persisted in their hardheaded outlook, if they were so ruled by spite and distrust that they would not accept a helping hand when it was offered, then they were doomed.

And unless he could turn the tables, so were those he loved most.

Chapter Ten

Zach King's right shoulder hurt something fierce. The war club had evidently struck a nerve, because he had lost some of the feeling in his arm. It tingled and throbbed, rendered momentarily useless.

But when he saw the Anasazi with the bow take aim at his mother, when he saw that she could not bring her rifle to bear in time, he grit his teeth and willed his right arm to move whether it wanted to or not.

He could not use his left hand. In it he held the bay's reins and the spent Hawken.

Zach nearly cried out as his right arm screamed in protest. By sheer willpower he wrapped his fingers around one of the big pistols at his waist. The Anasazi had the tip of the barbed shaft fixed on his mother's torso; another instant and the arrow would take wing. Shoving his arm outward, Zach thumbed back the hammer and fired.

In his condition, and with the bouncing of the bay,

Zach could not aim very well. He did the best he could. And while the shot did not have the immediate effect he wanted, it had the desired result.

The .55-caliber smoothbore belched smoke and lead. The warrior's fingers were starting to release the string when the ball, by sheer accident or the design of providence, hit the ash bow several inches above the Anasazi's knuckles. It splintered the wood, and the feathered shaft intended for Winona's breast instead fluttered erratically and embedded itself in the earth midway between them.

The Anasazi shook a fist at Zach and howled in fury.

Winona expressed her gratitude in the look she gave Stalking Coyote. Words were not necessary.

Shoshones by nature were passionate about life and deeply affectionate toward one another. As Nate has taken some time to learn, they expressed their affection more in actions than in words. Which was why, after they escaped the valley, once they were back home, Winona intended to do something special for her son as a token of her thanks. Maybe she would get him a new knife. Maybe a new saddle. Whatever she did, it would come from her heart, and mean more than words ever could.

Evelyn saw more warriors hurrying to cut them off and slapped her legs against her pony's sides. She was scared, awfully scared, but she did as her mother had taught her and did not let it show. "Courage is as important for a woman as for a man," Winona had once told her. "Just as you learn how to cook and sew, you must learn to be brave. Never shame yourself or your man by being a coward."

"But, Ma," Evelyn had said, recalling their run-in with a grizzly. "What if I can't help myself? What if I'm so frightened I can't think straight?"

"Don't let it show. As people grow, they learn to control their tempers, to control their tongues. Learning to control how you act when you are afraid is the same. The difference between a coward and a brave person is that cowards let their fear control them while the brave ones control their fear.''

So now Evelyn pushed her fright to the back of her mind, hunched forward, and rode like the wind.

The Anasazis fell behind. Winona did not feel truly safe until the trees closed around them. Slowing, she veered to the southwest, riding deeper into the woodland in the general direction of the horseshoe city. A glance at the sun showed they had several hours yet before the sun would set.

"What are we going to do next, Ma?" Zach asked. All the running and hiding they were doing did not fit his image of how a true warrior should act.

"What I have planned to do all along. We must find where the Anasazis are keeping your father. Then one of us will sneak in and get him out."

"I'll go," Zach immediately volunteered. When the other Shoshone boys heard about it, they would be green with envy.

"No. I will." Winona raised a hand to stifle her son's protest. "To pass for an Anasazi, you must dress like one. And we do not have the clothes their men wear." She touched her dress. "In the dark, I think I have a better chance of being mistaken for one of their own women."

"You don't know that for sure," Zach said sulkily. "We haven't seen any of their women close up. The Anasazis might catch you, too."

Winona knew why her son was so greatly upset, but she would not relent. Trying to lighten his mood, she grinned and said, "Then you will have the two of us to rescue."

Rubbing his sore shoulder, Zach rode on without comment. It was downright unfair, he reflected, that every time he had a chance to count more coup, his folks ruined it. They treated him as if he were Evelyn's age. If they kept it up, one of these days he was going to go off on his own, or maybe with a select group of friends, and prove to everyone beyond a shadow of a doubt that he was a worthy son of Grizzly Killer and a warrior in his own right.

In under an hour they came to the high crown of a long-unused series of terraces that overlooked the Anasazi city. A small herd of strange, deerlike animals was grazing on the high grass, and at their approach, fled into the forest.

Zach yearned to shoot one, but the shot would be heard below. He had some pemmican and jerky in a parfleche, enough to last several days, but neither could rival the taste of freshly roasted meat dripping with fat and grease.

After tethering their mounts, the three of them crawled to the rim and spied on their enemies. "Look for sign of your father," Winona said. "He should be the only one wearing buckskins." Even at that distance, her husband would stand out. But though they watched for hours, though they strained their eyes until the sun was perched on the lip of the western cliffs, they did not spot him.

"They must have Pa inside somewhere," Zach said, stating the obvious. "What if they never bring him outdoors?"

Winona was mulling that very problem. To search the entire city was the same as asking to be captured. They'd have to go from rooftop to door, peering into each and every opening.

Evelyn twisted to relieve a cramp in her arm. At the tree line stood one of the cute deerlike creatures they had seen earlier, a young one, contentedly grazing. It did not appear to be afraid of them or their horses. "Look, Ma," she whispered.

Turning, Winona saw the deer, and smiled. "If it comes closer, try to feed it some grass by hand."

The Lost Valley

Zach thought the idea was terrific. While his sister distracted it, he could grab the critter around the neck and slash its throat before it could let out a peep. Then he'd go back in the trees and light a small fire. His stomach growled in anticipation.

Just then the creature raised its dainty head and sniffed loudly. Its wide eyes swung toward the undergrowth. Tail flicking, ears erect, it took a few steps to one side, then to the other.

"It's acting scared," Evelyn said. "Why?"

The deer bolted, plunging into the wall of green and vanishing. They could not hear it, so quietly did it move. Winona started to turn back toward the slope when a hideous cry rent the shadowy terrain, a high-pitched bleat that swelled to a strangled shriek. Abruptly, the cry died.

"Something got it!" Evelyn said, and went to run to its aid.

"Be still," Winona said, gripping her daughter's wrist.

From the vegetation rose a loud crunch. There was no mistaking the sound for anything other than what it was: a bone being clamped onto by powerful jaws. More crunching ensued, along with low grunts.

The horses had caught the predator's scent and were prancing and nickering. Worst was the pony, which pulled against its tether in a panic.

"We have to shut them up," Zach said. He ran to do so before the thing that had caught the little deer got wind of the horses. Whatever was in there had to be big, and just might decide that one measly deer was not enough to satisfy its hunger.

Winona rose. "We must help your brother."

The horses were growing more agitated by the moment. The mare whinnied and tugged and stomped its hooves, even after Winona rubbed its neck and spoke soothingly. The loudest crunch yet nearly made the horse uncontrollable.

Mixed with the snap of bones was the rending of flesh and the smack of inhuman lips. Snorts and grunts punctuated the grisly feast. It was like listening to a grizzly eat, only louder, more ghastly.

Suddenly the sound of eating stopped. Winona clamped a hand over the mare's muzzle and Zach did likewise with the bay. Evelyn was a shade slow in covering the pony's, and her tardiness reaped a shrill nicker that was answered by a throaty, questioning growl.

New snapping noises arose. Not the snapping of bones, but the snap of tree limbs and the crackle of brush. Winona's breath caught in her throat. Whatever had devoured the red deer was coming toward them!

Nate King's fingers were unbearably sore. All bore cuts, some deeper than others. His left index finger was the worst, always bleeding and stinging, even after he ripped a strip from the hem of his hunting shirt and bandaged the laceration.

The pain had been worth it. In the hours since the Anasazis had quizzed him, he'd made wonderful progress. His hard toil had resulted in a hole the size of a melon. At his feet were piled the heavy stones he had removed, and a mound of dirt.

The room on the other side was unoccupied, but it might not be so much longer. Thanks to the light spilling in from above, Nate could see the many possessions that belonged to its occupants. Blankets, baskets, pots and other cooking utensils, clothes, and much more were neatly arranged around the quarters.

Nate guessed that whoever lived there would return along about sunset. That was when the tillers would come in from the fields, when warriors would come for their supper, when families would come back to their home. He had to get out of there before then.

Incentive was provided by a ladder bathed in waning

sunlight. If only he could reach it! Under cover of darkness, escaping would be easy. But there was a hitch, a hitch that might result in his prompt recapture. He had given his word to take the Ute boy and Pedro along, and he was not leaving without them.

Nate dug into the wall with renewed vigor. He had excavated two deep horizontal furrows, one a couple of feet above the other, and each a couple of feet long. Applying the sharp pottery shard to the top one, he scraped and pried and dug until he was almost through.

He was running out of time. The light was fading, the sky darkening. Soon, very soon, the sun would go down, and once that happened, once the fiery orb sank below the western rim of the mesa, it would be the same as snuffing out a lantern. The rooms would be plunged into inky gloom, and he would have to grope his way in the dark.

Of course, by then the occupants were bound to return. Nate set down the shard, stepped back, and smashed his right foot against the wall, between the furrows. Again and again he pounded, and he was rewarded by hairline fractures that spread with each blow.

Break, damn you! Nate mentally railed. His right foot grew sore, so he switched to his left. More cracks appeared, but not enough, nowhere near enough. Looping his left arm through the hole, he braced it against the opposite side of the wall, then pulled inward with all his strength. Mortar crumbled. Dirt cascaded in an ever-growing quantity. His muscles bulged, his chest heaved.

Brreak! Break! Break! Stepping back, Nate delivered another kick, throwing all of his weight into it. The mortar gave way completely and rocks clattered into both rooms. Bending, he squeezed into the gap. His shoulders made it through, but his chest snagged on the jagged edges. Wriggling would not free him. He pushed against the wall and gained a few inches, no more. He was caught like a beaver in a trap.

Voices above stilled his exertions. Nate heard footsteps. He glanced at the opening and tensed in dread that the silhouette of a person would appear. But whoever was up there walked on by.

The light was almost gone.

Nate applied himself in a frenzy, wrenching and tearing at the wall like a man gone berserk. His fingers bled profusely and his chest flamed with agony. He was beginning to despair of ever freeing himself when the portion of wall under him buckled. He had to throw both arms over his head to keep from cracking his noggin as he was spilled onto the floor.

Not wasting a second, Nate rose and ran to the ladder. Swiftly, he climbed, but he was only halfway up when more voices sounded and footsteps approached. Jumping down, he scrambled into a corner.

The room was now so dark that Nate could not see the collapsed wall from where he stood. Hopefully, neither would the occupants as they came down the ladder.

A woman laughed lightly and lowered her legs through the entrance. Descending, she chattered gaily, looking up, not at the floor. Behind her came a man. Tillers, to judge by their clothing, or lack of it. They were middle-aged, a married couple, Nate figured. Neither was armed, that he could see.

He needed a weapon. Recalling that there had been a broom propped in the corner, he probed along the wall and found it. The handle was short, thick, and heavy, sturdy enough to serve as a cudgel. He did not want to hurt the couple, but he'd be a fool to let them call out. He'd have every last Anasazi in the city down on his shoulders.

The woman reached the floor and turned. Spying the debris, she put a hand to her throat and spoke excitedly.

Her husband looked at the shattered wall, then jumped. Together they cautiously walked toward the hole.

Nate had a choice to make. They had their backs to him; he could drop them both before either knew he was there. Instead, he darted to the ladder and started up, taking two rungs at a stride. They could not help but hear him, and spun. The man took two bounds and grabbed his ankle.

Nate attempted to jerk his leg loose, but the Anasazi was as strong as a bull. A lifetime of toil had turned the man's sinews into solid iron. Nate swung the broom, slamming it against the Anasazi's temple hard enough to knock out most men. All the tiller did was grunt.

The wife leaped to her husband's side. Crying out, she clawed at Nate's other leg. Her weight, combined with the man's, unbalanced Nate. Since he could not hold on to the rung with both hands and still keep hold of the broom, he dropped it.

Clinging precariously as the ladder swiveled and threatened to dump him, Nate fought to climb higher. The Anasazis were intent on keeping him there, their nails digging into him like talons.

A sharp crack rent the room. The ladder was breaking. With a mighty heave, Nate gained the next rung. The woman lost her grip, but not her husband. Glancing around, Nate brought the sole of his foot crashing down on the man's nose. Cartilage crunched, and the Anasazi's fingers slipped off him.

Nate spurted to the top, vaulting onto the roof just as the ladder buckled and fell. He was out, but there was no cause to celebrate. For at that juncture the woman vented a scream that would do justice to a panther. Almost as if on cue, an Anasazi appeared on the next roof, a war club in hand.

Chapter Eleven

Without thinking, Winona King swung astride her skittish mare and prepared to race over the crown of the uppermost terrace. As she was lifting the reins, she hesitated. The sun had just relinquished the vault of sky above the mesa to a few twinkling stars, but it was not yet dark enough to conceal her and the children on the slopes below. The Anasazis might spot them.

Evelyn mounted her pony with difficulty. The terrified animal would not stand still. It nickered and pranced, never once taking its eyes off the wall of vegetation that separated them from whatever approached.

Zach was last to climb on, in case the thing attacked. He was between the trees and the others, so the creature was bound to focus on him first. The crackle and snap of brush being trampled grew louder and louder, and he could hear the beast's heavy breathing, like the wheezing of a bellows in a blacksmith's shop.

A dark shape materialized, the spectral outline of a

gargantuan bulk, and halted a stone's throw away. A tell-tale gleam among the leaves seemed to be an eye. Zach could feel it studying him, and a chill swept his body. He could not be positive, but he had a hunch it was one of the monsters that had wiped out the Ute hunting party. Maybe it was the very same monster.

Evelyn was too petrified to move a muscle. She had never seen anything so huge. To her, it was unspeakably evil. All the badness in the world, all the wickedness, all the vile things that should not be, were centered in that enormous shape.

Winona was filled with inexplicable loathing. She felt as if she were in the presence of an abomination of all that had ever been, an entity that had no business being alive and yet was, a being from the old times when Coyote first walked the earth. Her rifle was loaded and primed, but she could not bring herself to shoot for fear that she would only wound it and provoke it into attacking. Against a thing that immense, they would fare the same as the hapless Utes.

A rumbling growl warned that the creature might charge anyway. Winona saw it lumber a few yards to the north, saw what must be its head tilt in their direction. The rustle of leaves on alien skin was unnerving, as was the sibilant hissing that ensued. A slender object the length of her arm speared the twilight and was withdrawn. She was jolted to realize it must be the creature's tongue. The beast was testing the air as would a snake.

Zach definitely saw an eye fixed on him, an eye the size of a frying pan. An inky pool of brutish malevolence that tore into the depths of his being and ignited fear so potent he could not help trembling. Was this what the Utes had felt during their last moments? he wondered. The same unreasoning panic that gripped him?

The hissing continued, along with an odd regular swishing, as of something being rubbed back and forth over the forest floor. Its tail, Zach guessed.

Winona did not understand why the thing just stood there, watching them. Was it merely curious? Had the red deer satisfied its appetite? Or was it going to explode from the vegetation and overwhelm them before they got off a shot?

The creature answered her question by turning and moving off into the gathering night, its ponderous tread resembling muted drumbeats. Then the rending of limbs grew fainter and fainter, until at last the only sound was the sigh of the wind and the distant cry of a bird.

"What was it, Ma?" Evelyn breathed. "Is there anything like it where we live?"

"No, of course not," Winona said with confidence she did not feel. No one could say with authority what lurked in the remote vastness of the mountains. There were places so remote that no one had ever visited them, not red men nor whites, mysterious places, places reputed to be bad medicine, places better shunned than visited. In those hidden nooks might dwell creatures long gone from the rest of the world, creatures that clung tenaciously to life as if waiting for the day when the reign of man would end and their kind could spread out over the world again as they had in the dim past.

The thought made Winona uneasy, as if she had stumbled on a truth better left unknown. "Come," she announced, and rode along the summit to the south, to where the trees did not crowd the rim. To where they would have a few second's forewarning if something rushed out at them.

"What now?" Evelyn asked.

"We wait."

And wait they did, for another hour, until the terraces were cloaked in an inky mantle. It was an hour that further frayed their frazzled nerves, thanks to savagery gone amok in the forest.

The Lost Valley

The beasts claimed the night as their own. Again and again the verdant growth was punctured by fierce roars, unearthly howls, and bestial screeches. Night transformed the tranquil valley into a slaughter ground, a constant contest for survival between predators and prey, between hunters and hunted.

Winona did not let on that the din rattled her. The sounds were similar to those she was accustomed to outside the lost valley—similar, yet different. The cries were those of creatures she had never encountered, of animals unlike those that dwelled in the mountains and the plains, of animals probably unlike those found anywhere else.

Once a frenzied bleating broke out close at hand. It was the death cry of another red deer, or something like it. When the bleating died they heard loud thumping, then a roar to end all roars, a roar of triumph that drowned out all the other sounds in the valley. For the longest while after the roar died, not a peep was heard.

Toward the end of the hour a battle broke out between two meat-eaters. Their snarls and roars rose in a feral chorus amplified by the towering cliffs.

Winona was at a loss to explain why the Anasazis had chosen to live there, and why they stayed on. At night it was virtual suicide to be abroad in the woodland. In effect, the Anasazis were prisoners in their own city once the sun went down.

Maybe, Winona mused, the tribe liked it that way. The mist, the red wolves, the high ramparts were all barriers that kept the outside world at bay. Possibly the same was true of the dense forest and its nocturnal bloodletters: They were another barrier, certain death for anyone unwitting enough to roam the woods after dark.

Winona was glad when the moment came to mount and descend the terraces. She reined up halfway down, where Zach and Evelyn had a clear view in all directions and no one could come at them without being seen.

"You will wait here for me," she directed as he gave her reins to Stalking Coyote.

Zach did not like it, but he did not argue. "How long do we cool our heels? What if you're not back by dawn?"

"Then go into the trees and hide. It should be safe enough in the daytime."

Evelyn was not keen on being left alone. "Why can't we go with you?" she asked. "We'd be real quiet."

Winona verified that her rifle was loaded and primed. "There are bound to be sentries, little one. One person can slip in where three would find it hard."

"I want to be with you," Evelyn persisted. She could imagine all kinds of hideous creatures slinking out of the forest to devour them once her mother was gone.

Gently resting a hand on her daughter's shoulder, Winona said, "I know. And if it were safe, I would take you. But now you must be brave. Remember our talk earlier? You must control your fear, not let it control you." She nodded at her son. "Besides, Stalking Coyote will protect you. He is as brave as his father, and a fine shot."

Zach was flattered by the compliment. "Don't worry about us, Ma. Nothing will get her while I'm alive."

Winona kissed her daughter, squeezed her son's arm, and left, working steadily lower until she came to a road. The tilled terraces lay quiet under the starlight. None of the Anasazis were abroad.

On the valley floor the nightmarish sounds of the prowling beasts were faint. Evidently they confined themselves to the woods, perhaps because that was where the game hid to escape.

Her thumb on the Hawken's hammer, Winona jogged toward the city. The walls gleamed dully, in part from the starlight, in part from countless torches kept lit along the outer perimeter. Figures moved on top of the walls and in the plaza.

Winona tried not to dwell on the daunting challenge ahead. Locating her husband would be next to impossible, but she was not leaving the valley without him. To her right the lake glistened. Something splashed loudly. She turned to see what it was, when suddenly the ground shook violently under her feet.

It was a repeat of the afternoon, only this time it was worse. The valley floor convulsed and heaved. Winona could not stay on her feet. The road surged upward, pitching her onto her stomach.

Suddenly, directly in front of her eyes, the earth split, yawning wide. And as she looked on in rising horror, the ground under her fell away.

Nate King whirled and crouched. The Anasazis would not retake him without a fight. In the room below, the woman and the man were yelling loud enough to rouse the dead. Certainly loud enough to bring every Anasazi within earshot on the run.

The man on the next roof raised the war club, but not to throw it. "*Senor* King, is that you?"

A low parapet divided the two apartments. Nate leaped over it and clutched Pedro Valdez's arm. "It's me, hoss. What the devil are you doing here?"

"I came to help you escape," the Mexican said, with a nod at the ladder he had just lowered into the apartment in which the mountain man had been originally imprisoned. "But apparently you do not need my help."

"We're both getting out of here."

Or were they? The hollering had drawn the interest of Anasazis in the plaza below and on the walls above. Patches of torchlight reflected off warriors and others hurrying to investigate.

At the moment, Nate and Pedro were sheathed in

shadow and were safe from detection. But they would not be so for much longer. "Where can we hide?" Nate asked.

"There is nowhere they will not look," the blind vaquero said. "They will search the city from top to bottom."

Shouts on the level below spurred Nate into action. Grabbing Valdez's hand, Nate pulled him to the ladder. "Can you climb down without making any noise?"

"You want to go back into the room where they held you?"

Nate did indeed. It was the last place the Anasazi would think to look. Or so he hoped. "Can you or not?"

"Sí. I can be like a tiny mouse when I need to."

"Then follow me."

The apartment was inky black. Nate did not take his eyes off the opening in the north wall as he went down. The couple in the next room had not thought to light a lamp or torch yet. They were still bawling their lungs out.

At the bottom Nate coiled and waited. His new friend was true to his boast and made no noise. Snatching Pedro's wrist, Nate pulled him into a far corner and had him hunker. Then Nate ran to where he had left the frayed sack. As he groped for it, feet drummed overhead.

The tillers yelled louder, and whoever was up there answered. Nate dashed to Valdez, squatted, and draped the sack over their heads. Lifting the edge, he peeked at the collapsed wall. From the sound of things, the couple were telling those on the roof what had happened.

A head poked down from the overhead entrance, made a quick scrutiny, and was withdrawn. Someone barked orders. Footsteps pounded off in various directions.

"The search has begun," Pedro whispered. "Wakon-homin himself is leading it."

Light flared in the room next door. A person bearing

a torch came to the buckled wall and poked the torch past it. The glow cast by the crackling flames illuminated most of the floor but not the far corners, not the corner where the trapper and the vaquero were. Whoever held the torch snorted like an angry bull and turned away.

Soon the whole city thrummed with movement. Anasazis were constantly shouting, reporting, receiving instructions, as they hastened from door to door, apartment to apartment. Nate compared the situation to being caught in a hive of riled bees.

"My congratulations, *señor*," Pedro whispered after half an hour. "You are very sly, like the fox."

"We're still not out of danger," Nate reminded him. Which was the understatement of the century. To reach the jungle they must sneak from the city and cross a lot of open space. In broad daylight it would be impossible. So they must make their bid before sunrise, when the city might still be swarming with Anasazis.

"No matter what happens, my friend, I thank you for trying to save me," Pedro said solemnly. "But I ask you again to change your mind. I will only slow you down."

"It's whole hog or nothing at all."

A racket in the next apartment led Nate to believe that the couple had joined the hunt. The glow faded when they departed, leaving both rooms in total darkness. Nate could not see his fingers when he held them six inches in front of his nose.

Pedro touched his elbow. "I almost forgot, *señor*. I found the Ute boy."

"Nevava?"

"I do not know his name. He does not speak English or Spanish, and I do not speak his tongue. He is being held in the temple. The priests will use him as a helper. When he is older, if he proves he can be trusted, they will adopt him into the tribe."

"The temple? Is that the building by itself at the south-west corner of the plaza?"

"*Sí*. The kiva is there."

"The what?"

"A special place where the Anasazis worship. They pray there every day, and hold rites. There are other kivas in the city, smaller ones, not as important."

Nate would have liked to learn more about the religious aspect of the Anasazis' lives, but it had gotten quiet nearby. Now was as good a time as any to make their break. "Stay close to me," he cautioned, tugging at the blind man's sleeve.

They crept toward the ladder, Nate alert for obstacles his friend might trip over. His foot bumped a basket, and he kicked it aside. "When we reach the top we'll head straight for the temple."

"How will you get across the plaza?"

"I'll cross that bridge when I come to it." Nate had a half-baked plan. If he could get his hands on a blanket, he would throw it over him and trust in—

Suddenly Pedro grabbed his shirt. "*Señor*, do you feel it?" he anxiously asked.

"Feel what?" Nate responded, and the next instant the whole room shook as if it were being buffeted by cyclonic winds. But Nate knew better. He darted to the ladder and steadied it, saying, "Another earthquake! Hurry! We've got to get out of here!"

"Above us! Do you hear?"

Pedro's sensitive ears had registered the cracking and splintering of mortar and beams a second before Nate's had. Glancing up, Nate blinked as dust rained onto his head and into his eyes. A heartbeat later, a section of the roof caved in on them.

Chapter Twelve

Zachary King was honing the blade of his hunting knife when the earthquake hit. For a short while after his mother left them he had paced the rim of the terrace, worry gnawing at him like a beaver through bark. Deciding he needed to do something to take his mind off his folks, he had taken a whetstone from his possibles bag, sat facing the Anasazi city, and proceeded to sharpen his knife.

Evelyn had spread a blanket on the grass and curled into a ball. She was too upset to sleep, so she lay there fretting and wishing the family had never left home. She was not like her brother, who always craved excitement and adventure. Peace and quiet appealed to her more. Fondly, she recalled the many quiet evenings she had spent lying warm and toasty in front of the fireplace, her mother sewing or knitting, her father reading aloud.

She would give anything to be doing that now. No hostile Indians would be trying to kill them. Nothing would be trying to eat them. They would not be trapped in a strange place that reeked of evil. They would be happy, at their ease, content. Which was how life was meant to be.

"I don't think I'm ever going to go on one of these gallivants again," Evelyn announced.

"You will."

Her brother's blunt reply disturbed her. He was always so smug, always acting superior. "What makes you so sure?"

"Because you're glued to Ma. Where she goes, you go. If our folks were to take it into their heads to travel to Canada or the Pacific Ocean, you'd be right at their side."

It was the truth, but Evelyn was not going to openly admit as much. "Maybe I would, maybe I wouldn't," she hedged. *Just because he's older, he thinks he knows everything.*

"Oh, please," Zach said while stroking the edge of his blade at the proper angle across the whetstone. "What else would you do? Stay home by yourself?"

"I could always live with Uncle Spotted Bull and Aunt Morning Dove." Evelyn had him there. Her mother's brother and his wife would be glad to look after her for a spell. They were always delighted when the family came to visit.

Evelyn enjoyed her yearly stays in the Shoshone village, but it was not the same as being at home. She did not much like it that the men got to go off and do all the hunting and such while the women were expected to do all the chores around the lodges. Her aunt was always cooking or mending or skinning or curing hides and never seemed to have much time to relax and enjoy life.

Secretly, Evelyn harbored a desire to venture east of the Mississippi one day and visit a big city. Her father had told her all about them, about the shops where a woman could buy pretty dresses and hats and anything else she needed. He'd told her about the theater and concerts and gay parties where people danced the night away.

Evelyn's fondest possession was a catalogue her pa had picked up somewhere. It showed all sorts of items a person could purchase, everything from clothes to plows. Many an evening she had spent flipping its pages, fascinated by the many strange and wondrous marvels on sale. On many an afternoon she had daydreamed about what it would be like to live in a lodge made of brick or stone, to have servants wait on her hand and foot, to go for strolls wearing the latest in fashion. *Wouldn't that be grand!*

Evelyn had grown drowsy. Closing her eyes, she listened to the wail of an animal in torment. Suddenly she felt the ground shake and she sat bolt upright. "Zach!"

"It's another quake," Zach said, and began to rise. He was on one knee when the whole terrace bucked and heaved like a mustang. His Hawken lay on the grass at his side, and he made a grab for it, afraid it would slide down the slope. To his consternation, a second later his legs were jarred out from under him and *he* tumbled over the brink.

"Zach!" Evelyn yelled, trying to rise. She was thrown onto her back, unhurt but terribly scared. The horses shared her fear, for they were whinnying and rearing. She rolled onto her side and saw her pony bolt, racing pell-mell up the slopes toward the forest.

"No!" Evelyn shoved onto her hands and knees, but that was the best she could do until the upheaval ended a minute later. She did not move right away, afraid it was just a lull.

At the bottom of the terrace, Zach slowly rose, rubbing a sore spot on his ribs. He had dropped his whetstone when he fell and nearly stabbed himself as he tumbled.

Sheathing his knife, he started back up. "Evelyn, are you all right?"

"Yes, but the pony ran off."

"Drat." Zach reached the top and spotted his whetstone. Shoving it into his possibles bag, he picked up his Hawken. "Which way?"

Evelyn pointed at the black fringe of vegetation visible high above them. "We have to go after him."

"We'll do no such thing," Zach responded. "Ma told us to stay put, and that's exactly what we're going to do."

"But what if one of those monsters gets wind of him? He'll be eaten."

"It's his own fault for being so stupid. I always said that critter was too mule-headed for its own good."

Evelyn was shocked her own brother could be so coldhearted. "You don't care if George Washington winds up dead?" She had given the pony that name because she had always been fond of the first president after hearing about his life from her pa. Her favorite part was where young George owned up to chopping down a cherry tree.

"What a dumb name for a horse," Zach said for the umpteenth time as he stepped to the other animals to calm them.

"Is not." Pouting, Evelyn moved to her mother's mare. "Fine. If you won't lend a hand, I'll catch George myself. Give me a boost."

Zach knew how stubborn his sister could be when she set her mind to something. "Look. I'd like to help you. Really and truly. But what if Pa and Ma come back and find us and the horses gone?"

"That's easy. Leave the stallion and the mare here, hobbled. That way they can't wander off. We'll take your bay and be back before you know it."

The suggestion made sense, but Zach balked. His sister

did not seem to realize that if they followed the pony into the forest, the pony wasn't the only thing that might wind up in the belly of one of those huge beasts.

"Please," Evelyn pleaded. "The longer we take, the harder it will be to catch him."

She had another point. Reluctantly, Zach took a pair of hobbles from his pa's parfleche. "Have it your way. But I hope we don't regret this."

"Don't worry. We won't."

Winona King flung herself to the right as the gaping earth yawned wide to swallow her. She landed on her shoulder and rolled, then kept on rolling, over and over and over, until she was confident she was in the clear. Half dizzy, she stood.

The earth had stopped buckling. A chasm as wide as a Shoshone lance had rent the middle of the road. She thought of the children, but figured they would be safe enough. From what she could see, the terraces had not split apart as the valley floor had.

Behind her a peculiar gurgling erupted. Winona pivoted and was startled to behold the surface of the lake foam and bubble like soup in a cauldron. Only, it was not giving off steam or smoke. She moved closer and saw that the water along the shore was moving, swirling parallel with the shoreline.

Puzzled but unwilling to waste more time, Winona turned toward the city. She stopped cold when the lake made a moaning sound like a woman in labor. The water was flowing faster in the same circular pattern, while in the center it roiled and churned.

Again she started to leave, but surprise rooted her in place. The lake was shrinking! Right before her eyes the water level was falling rapidly. But that could not be, she told herself.

Now all the water was in motion, flowing like a river,

in a great circle. In the middle the surface was parted as if by an invisible hand, forming a funnel. A sucking sound replaced the moans, a sound like that made by a foal sucking on its mother's teat, magnified many times.

At last Winona understood. In her cabin she had a sink, courtesy of her considerate husband. At the bottom was a drain that emptied into a bucket. Whenever she let the water out after cleaning dishes, it swirled in the same manner as the lake and sometimes made the same sucking noises.

The earthquake was to blame. It had cracked the lake bed just as it had split the road, and now the water was being drawn into the depths of the earth. Once it was gone, what would the Anasazis do? How would they survive? Without water, their crops would wither. Without water, they would soon die of thirst.

Winona did not linger to witness the outcome. She had Nate to think of. Cradling her rifle, she hurried to the south.

Nate King threw his arms over his head to ward off the falling stones and mortar, but it was like trying to ward off an avalanche. Some of the stones were as big as melons. They pummeled him, gouging flesh, battering bones, and nearly drove him to his knees.

Pedro cried out. Nate tried to go to him, but a chunk of wall more than two feet wide smashed onto his shoulder and the world blinked out.

How long Nate lay unconscious he could not say, although it could not have been more than a few minutes. Dust filled the air, getting into his nose, his mouth. He fought back a sneeze and tried to sit up, but couldn't. His legs were pinned under the chunk that had fallen on him. Sliding his hands underneath, he pushed, straining against the weight. Inch by gradual inch, the slab slid off.

There was no sensation in his right leg. Dreading it

might be broken, Nate rose gingerly, applying his full weight only when he was erect. His thigh hurt abominably, but the feeling returned after he pumped the leg a few times.

The rest of his body had not fared much better. His shirt was ripped, his chest was cut and bruised, his arms bore welts and slash marks, and his left shoulder hurt if he so much as twitched it. But his own welfare did not concern him.

"Pedro?"

The vaquero lay under a pile of debris, his legs and one arm all that could be seen. Bending, Nate tore into the pile, flinging it to the right and the left, heedless of the noise he made.

"Pedro?"

There was no answer. Nate's hands fairly flew. He came to part of a wide beam and gripped it. Bunching his shoulders, he raised one end. It was like trying to raise a ten-ton boulder. He'd expected the beam to be heavy but nowhere near as heavy as it was. As he swung it clear, his left foot almost slipped out from under him. A glance showed why.

Trickling across the floor were rivulets of blood. Nate let the beam fall and knelt. "Pedro?" he said softly. Valdez was on his back, breathing raggedly, a jagged cavity in his chest. Nate touched the men's cheek.

Groaning, the vaquero stirred to life, his sightless eyes fixed on the shadowed ceiling. "*Señor* King? Is that you? What happened?"

"Another quake." Nate leaned low to examine the extent of the wound. Sorrow racked him, and he wanted to beat on the beam with his fists.

"I feel so weak. My head swims." Pedro attempted to sit up but could not. Wincing, he would have collapsed if Nate had not caught him.

"Lie still."

"How bad is it?"

Nate hesitated, unwilling to impart the truth and just as unwilling to lie. "You need to rest," he hedged.

Pedro Valdez was no fool. "That bad," he said forlornly. His Adam's apple bobbed. "I guess I will never see Mexico again, eh? Never see a golden sun rise over the desert of Sonora, or the beauty of the Sierra Madres."

"Maybe the Anasazis can heal you," Nate said. "I'll go fetch them."

The vaquero's hand groped upward and wrapped around Nate's arm. "You will do no such thing, *amigo*. They would only take you captive again, and this time maybe they would bind you." A coughing fit seized him, and his face flushed purple. When it subsided, he gasped for air, rasping, "It is no use anyway. I am fading. I can feel it."

Nate was at a loss to know quite what to say. They had not been friends long enough for a deep bond to have grown, but he liked Valdez immensely and was profoundly sad. "There might be some water in the next room. Hold on. I'll go see."

"No," Pedro said, and coughed violently again. Froth appeared at the corners of his mouth. "There is something more important. Promise me you will get word to Jonathan Levi of San Antonio, as I asked once before. Have him tell my parents what happened."

"I give my word."

"Bueno, bueno," Pedro said, practically whispering. For a while he was still, so still that the mountain man pressed fingers over his wrist to verify he was still alive. Inhaling loudly, Pedro smacked his lips and said, "Who would have thought it? That I would end my days like this?" He laughed bitterly, inducing another spurt of coughs and wheezes.

"You shouldn't talk."

"Why not? In a little bit I will be gone. I cannot move

116

and I cannot see. All I can do is talk. If that is the only joy left to me, then talk I will." His hand tightened on Nate. "It hurts so much. I would scream, but it would bring the Anasazis down on you."

"They should pay for their atrocities."

"No, *señor*. They do only what they must. Once, I hated them more than any man has ever hated anyone. But now I feel only pity. My time is short, but so is theirs. They are the last of their kind, and soon there will come a day when they will be no more." Pedro could barely voice the words, but the simple exertion took its toll in the form of spasms that had him gulping for every breath.

The trapper cradled the vaquero's head in his lap. Presently the convulsions ended and Pedro tilted his head upward.

"Do you smell the night air? How fresh it is, like a garden of flowers. And that music! Where is it coming from?"

Nate sniffed but did not detect a fragrant scent. Nor did he hear music. Outside, the city was in turmoil, the Anasazis hollering all over the place, the bedlam punctuated by screams and the drumming of feet. "I still think I should find you some water."

Pedro did not respond. Nate placed a hand on the blind man's chest, then probed for a pulse. Sighing, he lowered the vaquero to the floor and slowly rose. "You deserved better."

A harsh yell close by sparked Nate into dashing to the buckled wall and over it into the next apartment. The roof was intact. The new ladder that had been lowered so the tillers could join the search was unscathed. Nate scaled it swiftly, springing out onto the roof without looking to make sure that the coast was clear.

It was a mistake.

Not six feet away stood a husky warrior.

Chapter Thirteen

Evelyn King had never been so scared in her life. As she and her brother neared the crest of the uppermost terrace, blind panic swelled and she came close to changing her mind. As much as she cared for George Washington, she was deathly afraid to venture into the forest after him.

The woodlands were still and quiet, but that did not deceive her. The monsters were in there, many of them, waiting and hungry. Swallowing, she bent to see Zach, whose face seemed paler than usual. "Why isn't there any noise?" she whispered.

"The quake must be to blame. It scared them."

The notion that the monsters could be scared was so novel that Evelyn blinked in surprise. It made them less scary, somehow.

Zach reined up at the crest. Every instinct he had screamed at him to turn around and ride like a bat out of Hades, but his sister was counting on him and he did not want to let her down. She loved that stupid pony as much

118

as he loved his pet wolf. Besides, going in after it was what his pa would do.

In that respect Zachary King was no different from youths all over the world. He measured his performance in life by the standard set by his father. He wanted to shoot as well as his father did, ride as well, track as well—in short, do everything exactly the same, or perhaps a shade better.

So now, with a murky maze of benighted vegetation looming before him, Zach held his Hawken close to his chest and kneed the bay. He listened for the sound of the pony going off through the brush but heard nothing, absolutely nothing. Even the breeze had died.

Evelyn had her arms around her brother's waist, and she tightened them as the undergrowth closed around them. Dark shadows hemmed them in, shadows that seemed to flit and leer, although she knew that could not be the case. Her nerves were to blame. She remembered what her mother had said about controlling her fears and steeled herself to be brave.

Zach paid particular attention to the bay. Its sense of hearing and smell were far sharper than his. If anything came near them the horse would know before he did. When its ears suddenly shot erect and its head swung to the right, he halted. In the distance a wolfish howl put an end to the eerie quiet. As the last reverberating notes faded, others took up the refrain. Somewhere to the east a behemoth roared. Somewhere to the north a victim squealed in torment.

Evelyn shivered, even though she was not cold. The forest was a bad place, a wicked place. Clearing her throat, she hollered, "George Washington! Where are you!"

Zach twisted so abruptly that he nearly knocked his sister off. "Hush!" he snapped. "What in the world has

119

gotten into you? Now everything that's out there knows right where we are.''

"Sorry," Evelyn said sincerely, mortified by her mistake. She had only intended to lure George Washington back. Sometimes he came when she called, but not always. As her pa once mentioned, the pony was an uppity cuss.

Zach rode on, avoiding inky areas and thickets and anywhere a predator might spring on them from concealment. The crack of a twig caused him to draw rein again. A ghostly shape was threading through the trees. Fear gripped him until he saw that the animal was small, and that it was moving away from them, not toward them. He smiled when he recognized it as one of the red deer so common in the valley.

Evelyn saw the deer too, and sympathy gushed from her like water from a geyser. It was unfair for the poor little things to have to spend their entire lives on the run from creatures that would rend them limb from limb. She never had understood why God saw fit to create animals that ate other animals. To her way of thinking, the world would be a lot better place if there were no suffering, whether for wild things or for people.

The deer dashed off, and Zach goaded the bay onward. The vegetation was so dense, the night so dark, that he began to fully appreciate how hopeless their task was. Finding the pony would be as hard as finding the proverbial needle in a haystack. But he had given his word to his sister, and his pa said that men always kept their word, no matter what.

Farther on, a wide clearing broadened ahead. In the center, grazing, were a number of creatures Zach had never seen before. They were short and squat, with snouts the shape of pie plates and gleaming tusks that jutted from their bottom jaws. Hideous beasts, but he figured they posed no threat. He stopped anyway, wary of the damage those tusks could do to the bay's legs if the things charged.

Suddenly the biggest one lifted its snout and sniffed. It was facing away from Zach. Whatever scent it had caught came from something on the other side of the clearing. The tusked critter grunted, its squiggly tail flapped, and then it let out a piercing screech and whirled. Instantly all nine of them bolted, fleeing in the opposite direction from whatever had spooked them.

Unfortunately, that put the bay directly in their path. Zach tried to rein into the brush, but the tuskers were quicker than he gave them credit for being. Squealing and snorting, they were on the horse in the blink of an eye and the one in the lead, the biggest one, the brute to blame for starting the stampede, slashed at the bay's forelegs.

Winona King was mildly surprised to find no sentries had been posted close to the Anasazi city. Nor did she see any men high on the outer walls, as she had earlier.

To judge by the racket she heard, the city was in chaos. Yells and shouts and screams hinted at utter bedlam.

Tucked at the waist, Winona sprinted to the northeast corner of the horseshoe. Once safe among the shadows, she crept toward the plaza, keeping her back to the wall. Above her it reared some thirty feet, lowering by degrees the closer she grew to the central open area.

She was midway when she noticed a wide crack, almost wide enough for her to slip through. From within wafted a musty odor, and she thought that she could hear someone softly crying.

Going on, Winona came to the end of the wall and peered around it. She did not know what she expected to find, but certainly not a city in smoldering ruins. The earthquake had devastated it. Roofs had buckled, walls collapsed. The central stairway was a shambles. More wide cracks laced nearly every dwelling, forming a spiderweb pattern that covered the city from bottom to top. Smoke rose from some of the rooftop openings, mostly tendrils, but in a few places choking black clouds billowed out.

The high building that was set apart from the rest had suffered the worst. Two-thirds of the north wall was gone, lying in crumbled piles. The east wall had partially given way. Flames were shooting from the roof, flaring bright red and orange and illuminating the tragic spectacle below.

Many Anasazis had been hurt or mortally stricken. Falling walls and heavy debris had crushed them where they stood. Bodies were scattered at the base of the wide stairs and on many of the shattered steps above. The living were doing what they could for the fallen, moving from body to body to check for signs of life. Some Anasazis, though, were in a state of shock. They drifted aimlessly, arms limp at their sides, their faces as blank as the slate Nate had bought for schooling the children. Wisps of smoke hovered over the scene, writhing and twisting like vaporous snakes.

Winona was at a loss to know what to do next. How, in the midst of all that, was she to find her husband?

Suddenly an Anasazi stepped past the end of the wall and halted right in front of her. She automatically brought up the Hawken, but she did not fire. The man was staring through her, not at her. In his arms he held a child of ten or twelve, a boy whose rib bones stuck out from a smashed chest. Both the man and the boy were covered in blood.

The Anasazi mumbled a few words, turned, and shuffled off.

Winona slowly rose. Maybe finding Nate was not as hopeless as it appeared. She was sorry the Anasazi had been afflicted so, but the quake had provided her with a golden opportunity. The Anasazis were too preoccupied to pay much attention to a lone woman wandering among them. Or so she fervently hoped.

Lowering her rifle so it was flush against her leg, Winona boldly strode into the plaza. She moved as the man had been moving, in a slow shuffle, pretending to be in the same stunned state, her head bowed. Peeking out from under her eyebrows, she scanned the honeycomb. Her man was nowhere to be seen.

Winona roved from east to west and back again. More and more smoke was spilling from the high building and spreading out over the city. It helped her in one respect since it cloaked her in an acrid fog, but it hindered her in another since soon she could not see even the lowest level of apartments.

The city reminded her a little of St. Louis. Nate had taken her there once, years ago. The stone buildings had been a source of awe. The whites' penchant for sticking down roots in one spot and never leaving it the rest of their lives had amazed and mystified her.

The Shoshones were always on the go. Villages were routinely packed onto travois and moved to new locations during the course of each year. Staying in one place more than a couple of moons was just not practical. Game was soon depleted, forcing the hunters to range farther and farther afield. Forage for the large horse herds became scarce. And, too, their enemies could strike more often if they stayed at one site for too long.

Winona's musing came to an end, and she looked up. Nearby were several women gathered around a dead man. She had drifted too close to them. Now she veered to give the group a wide berth and saw one of the Anasazi women gaze in her direction. Lowering her head, she walked more briskly, thankful for a column of smoke that drifted between them.

Glancing back, Winona saw the woman following. The

Anasazi's suspicions had been aroused. Increasing her pace a bit, Winona made for the east side of the plaza. She resisted an impulse to break into a run.

Maybe it would have been better if she had. For seconds later the Anasazi jabbed a finger at her and started yelling shrilly.

The warrior saw Nate King at the exact instant that Nate saw him. The man's reflexes were astounding. In three swift strides he closed in, elevating a war club to bash out Nate's brains.

Pivoting, the mountain man drove a brawny fist into the Anasazi's gut, doubling the warrior over. A knee to the jaw lifted him clear off the ground and dumped him on his back. Gamely, the warrior sought to rise while wildly swinging the club to keep Nate at bay.

Worried that more Anasazis would pounce on him at any moment, Nate dodged the club, slipped in under the man's long arm, and delivered a punch to the chin. Coming as it did on the heels of the previous blow, it folded the warrior like a piece of paper. Without a sound the Anasazi dropped onto the roof and was still.

Nate whirled, fists ready, but no other warriors were in his proximity. Taking a few steps toward the plaza, he discovered why. Widespread destruction had left the city a shadow of its former self. Dead and wounded—too many to count—littered the roofs, the stairs, the main plaza.

Recollecting that Pedro had told him the Ute boy was being held in the temple, Nate swatted some smoke aside and saw the demolished building. Sheets of flame had engulfed the upper levels. From the main entrance and side doors spilled refugees, many hacking uncontrollably.

There was a very real chance Nevava was no longer alive, yet that never gave Nate pause. Running to the edge of the roof, he saw the ladder that had been propped against it lying on the ground.

The drop was about twelve feet. Gripping the rim, Nate lowered himself over the side, dangled, and dropped. As he alighted, a cloud of smoke enveloped him. Landing on the balls of his feet, he tucked into a roll that brought him up in a crouch. Before he could straighten, a heavy blow slammed him between the shoulder blades and he was pitched onto his stomach.

Scrabbling onto his knees, Nate twisted just as a lean Anasazi with a knife thrust at his neck. Jerking aside saved his life—but he was safe only for the moment. The warrior waded in, cold steel flashing.

Nate lurched upright and frantically backpedaled. The smoke was so thick that he could barely see his adversary, so thick that his next breath seared his lungs with burning pain. He succumbed to a coughing fit, making it more difficult to keep dodging.

Suddenly the warrior dived, his free arm wrapping around the trapper's legs. With a powerful heave, they both were down, side by side, the warrior spearing his weapon at the mountain man's throat again and again.

Nate blocked, ducked, shifted, doing anything and everything to evade the onslaught. Taking the offensive, he grabbed the Anasazi's wrist and wrenched. His aim was to make the man drop the knife, but the warrior gritted his teeth and held on to it.

The smoke had grown steadily heavier. Since he could not disarm the Anasazi, Nate resorted to another tactic. Pushing the man with all his might, he leaped to his feet and scooted into the thick of the gray veil. He had to hold a hand over his mouth and nose, and breathe shallowly, in order not to cough and give his position away.

Cries, wailing, and screams swirled around the plaza, but in the center of the smoke the only sound Nate could hear was the pounding of his own temples. He turned this way and that, poised to defend himself. For all his diligence, though, the Anasazi caught him off guard; the knife streaked out of the smoke, nearly severing his jugular. That it didn't was through no effort on his part. The warrior misjudged the distance and missed.

Nate lashed out, connecting with a solid right. Recovering immediately, the Anasazi drove the tip of his blade down and in, going for the groin. Nate flung his legs wide, saw the knife pass between them.

All the warrior had to do was twist to either side to slice into Nate's thigh. To prevent that, and to give the Anasazi something else to occupy him, Nate flicked two fingers into his eyes.

Blinking furiously, the warrior retreated. Nate pressed the advantage he had by leaping behind the Anasazi and tripping him. As the man fell, Nate seized the knife arm in both hands and twisted sharply, throwing his entire weight into it. There was an audible crack. The Anasazi cried out and sagged.

Nate made short shrift of him, a flurry of punches finishing the fight. Scooping up the knife, Nate rotated, seeking to get his bearings. The smoke was thinning, and he could see the outline of a building a ways off. Was it the temple?

The mountain man started forward but took only two strides. Another Anasazi was rushing toward him. Unwilling to be delayed any longer, Nate cocked his arm. The smoke briefly thickened again, hiding the warrior, but Nate had gauged the man's speed well, and when a shadowy shape materialized in front of him, he was ready.

Nate's left hand closed on a shirt. His right hiked on high for a killing stroke. In another fraction of a second he struck. It was then, as the knife swooped down, that the smoke parted, and he saw it was not a buckskin shirt he held but a buckskin dress. And the upturned face so close to his was not that of an Anasazi—but his wife's.

Chapter Fourteen

It was the bay, not Zach, that saved them from the tuskers. As the big one bore down on them and slashed at the bay's knee, the horse's hoof flicked out, bowling it over. The rest of the herd slanted to the right or the left to go around. Unhurt, the big tusker leaped up and hastened after its companions, the crackle of brush fading rapidly.

"What was that all about?" Evelyn wondered.

Zach had a hunch he knew, and his gut balled into a knot. The night had grown unusually quiet. Then the bay snorted, its ears swiveling forward. Another couple of seconds and Zach heard it, too, the heavy tread of ponderous steps, the rhythmic *stomp-stomp-stomp* of something coming toward them, something enormous.

Evelyn was terrified to her core. "Get us out of here," she whispered, her nails digging into her brother's sides.

"Hush." Zach felt that staying perfectly still and making no noise was their best bet. The thing might not notice them, especially since the wind had died. Across the clearing, he saw a sapling bend and a massive form rear skyward nine or ten feet. He could not see it clearly, but what he did see was enough to change the blood in his veins to ice. It was almost manlike, with a huge misshapen head and sloped shoulders three times as broad as those of a typical man. Rumbling deep in a chest that must be as big around as five barrels, the thing swiveled from side to side, scouring the clearing.

The bay did not twitch a muscle, for which Zach was grateful. His sister was rigid against his back and did not let out a peep. The creature turned to the south and started to walk off, and Zach smiled.

Suddenly the thing halted and swung toward the clearing again. Zach did not understand why until he felt a breeze—against the back of his head. The monstrosity tilted its own head to test the air. In profile, the silhouette revealed a high conical forehead, wide, thick brows, and almost no neck. The protruding jaw sloped directly into its broad shoulders.

The rumbling became an ominous growl.

Zach did not linger another instant. The breeze had betrayed them and the thing knew right where they were. Hauling on the reins, he wheeled the bay and fled, crying, "Hang on tight, sis!"

Evelyn was too petrified to do anything else. A glance showed the creature barreling into the clearing, crossing it in four long leaps, and plowing into the undergrowth in pursuit. "Hurry!" she screeched. "It's after us."

Zach was doing the best he could, but there were so many trees and boulders and dense pockets of brush to be avoided that he could not bring the bay to a full gallop. A trot was as fast as he dared go. And as if that were not bad enough, low limbs lashed at him, branches tried to gouge his eyes or rip his face. He was constantly ducking and dodging and having to divert his gaze from the terrain ahead, which compounded the risk of a misstep or a collision. Should that occur, the thing would be on them in a twinkling.

It was incredibly fast for its bulk. Smashing through brush and plowing over small trees, the loathsome horror gained swiftly. Soon it was close enough for Evelyn to see its glinting eyes and hear its raspy breaths. The creature had an ungainly, rolling gait, due in part to the fact that its front legs appeared to be considerably longer than its rear ones. Yet despite that physical quirk, it narrowed the gap.

Zach veered sharply to go around a boulder, and the bay had to slacken its speed ever so slightly in order to adjust to the abrupt change.

The monstrosity had been waiting for just such a moment. Evelyn screamed as it hurtled at them and a hairy paw or hand thrust at her face. She felt something brush her hair and closed her eyes, afraid she would be yanked off and devoured. But just then the bay put on a spurt of speed. Anxious seconds went by. Evelyn fanned her courage and opened her eyes again to find that the creature had lost ground and was losing more each second.

"We're getting away!" she cried.

Zach would not believe they were safe until the thing was lost in the night. Goading the bay on, it occurred to him that he had lost all sense of direction. He did not know whether they were heading west, south, or north. No sooner did the question cross his mind than the bay burst from the woodland onto the top terrace.

Evelyn patted him on the back. "You did it," she said, amazed at their hairbreadth escape. She made a mental note to have more confidence in her brother in the future. Sure, he was obnoxious at times, as all boys could be, but he wasn't all bad.

Zach did not stop on the crest. Racing over it, he galloped down the slopes and was halfway to where they had left the stallion and the bay when an animal hove out of the darkness on their right. Thinking it was another meat-eater, he shifted to bring his Hawken to bear. His surprise on recognizing the animal was matched only by his anger at the peril it had put them in.

"Damn stupid pony," Zach said, reining up.

Evelyn squealed in delight and vaulted off the bay. Her pony was peacefully munching on grass, unruffled by the din in the forest. "George Washington!" she said as she threw her arms around his neck and kissed him below the ear. "You had us worried to death."

"Speak for yourself," Zach grumbled. "Me, I couldn't care less if the stupid critter wound up as worm food."

Evelyn grasped the pony's reins and turned. "You can be so mean, you know that? After all we went through, you should be happy George is alive."

"That's just it. We wouldn't have gone through what we just did if not for that dumb pet of yours." Zach glanced toward the upper terraces. "Now, quit jawing and climb on. The thing that was after us might follow our scent."

"Ma said those things mainly stay in the woods, remember?"

"Mainly," Zach emphasized. "And doesn't Pa like to say there are exceptions to every rule?"

Her brother had a point there. Evelyn mounted and patted her pony's neck. "By the way," she mentioned as she trailed the bay lower, "don't think I didn't hear that cussword you used. Pa will want to hear of it."

Zach twisted and glared at her. His father was a stickler for never using bad language in mixed company. Most of the mountain men had a flair for colorful speech and could "cuss rings around a tree," as Shakespeare McNair once put it. Some even did so in front of women, but his pa did not approve of the practice.

130

It had only been a year or so ago that Zach made the mistake of swearing in front of his mother. His pa had set him down and said, "When you're with other men, son, having a rollicking good time swapping lies and guzzling liquor, then cussing might be in order. But when you're with a lady, if you're so lazy that you can't say what has to be said without using cusswords, then you might as well keep your mouth shut."

"It was only a 'damn,' " Zach now told his sister in his defense. "You'd tell on me after all I just did for you?"

Evelyn was going to say that he deserved it for all the times he had teased her and played tricks on her, but the hurt in his tone gave her pause. He had saved their lives, after all. And he had gone in search of her pony even though he despised George Washington. "That makes two bad words," she said impishly, and when he puffed out his cheeks like an irate chipmunk, she said quickly, "But no, I won't tell on you. Not this time, anyway."

Zach's anger deflated and he nodded in approval. "For once you're showing some sense, sis. Not bad for a girl."

"Since when do you have something against girls?" Evelyn could not resist saying. "I saw how you were making cow eyes at Yellow Sky the last time we were with the Shoshones."

Yellow Sky was the pretty daughter of a prominent warrior. Zach had given her a small folding knife as a gift. In return, one evening as she returned from the river bearing water, she had let him sneak a kiss. He blushed at the memory and faced front. "You're imagining things again. Girls do that a lot."

Evelyn knew better, but she did not make an issue of it. She had George Washington back and she was content. Or as content as she could be with her mother and father missing. Where were they? she asked herself. Had something happened to them?

131

* * *

The answer to that question lay in the devastated Anasazi city.

Nate King's knife was inches from his wife's heart when he checked its plunge. All else was forgotten as he swept her into his arms and held her close, inwardly quaking at how close he had come to slaying the woman who meant everything to him, the woman he loved more than life itself. "Darling," he breathed. "I didn't know it was you."

"I certainly hope not," Winona quipped, sensing how deeply upset he was. She blamed herself for the incident, since she had recognized him as she was running through the smoke and should have called out instead of rushing to embrace him.

Winona recalled the reason she had been running, and urgently peeled herself from her husband's arms. "Anasazis are after me."

Nate looked up and saw dim figures gliding toward them. Grabbing his wife's wrist, he backed into the thickest of the smoke and ran to the right a dozen yards. Crouching, he pulled her down beside him and impulsively kissed her on the lips. "That will have to do until we get home," he whispered.

His romantic nature was an undying source of wonder for Winona. He was forever bringing her flowers and trinkets and whatnot, and lavishing her with finer things he obtained at one of the frontier forts. Many of her friends had told her it was unusual for a man to be so romantic; their own husbands seemed to lose more and more of that special quality the longer the couples were together.

Winona counted herself fortunate she had married a man who was so attentive and who daily treated her as if she was special.

Babbling voices and the patter of moccasin-shod feet

heralded her pursuers, almost a dozen swarthy warriors and Anasazi women who had come on the run when that first woman started yelling. They plunged into the smoke and spread out, swatting at it in a vain bid to see.

Stooped low to the ground, Nate could see their feet and the lower portion of their legs, but that was all. The smoke had grown thicker, a reminder that the temple was rapidly being consumed and might well burn to the ground—and that the Ute boy, Nevava, might be inside.

Rising partway, Nate drew Winona after him as he stealthily moved in the direction he hoped the temple lay. The babbling voices diminished in their wake, and he was beginning to think they had eluded the searchers when a man appeared out of the wispy fog, a stout Anasazi who wore a short plumed headdress and had a red blanket draped over his shoulders.

The man opened his mouth to cry out. Nate's fist silenced the shout, and the Anasazi tottered. Wading in, Nate rained a flurry of jabs and punches that drove the man to the ground, sprawled senseless.

Winona had covered the Anasazi in case he resorted to a weapon. She scanned the smoke as her husband donned the red blanket, and when he beckoned, she jogged at his side, out into the open.

The bedlam, if anything, was worse. Fires were spreading on all levels. Panicked women and children milled aimlessly. Some of the men were striving their utmost to snuff the flames, but they could not douse them fast enough.

No one paid much attention to the Kings. It helped that patches of smoke were everywhere, providing plenty of cover. They could not go ten feet without encountering one. As Nate barged through yet another swirling cloud, he saw the temple clearly again. Up close, the destruction was ten times as bad as he had imagined.

Wide cracks covered the outer walls. The lintel over

David Thompson

the entrance was split in half and ready to collapse at any
moment. Giant flames rimmed the roof and shot from
upper windows. Inside, screams and sobs and hysterical
raving testified to the pandemonium.

Turning to Winona, Nate said, "I'm going in after the
Ute boy. Stay here until I get back."

"No."

That was all there was to it. Nate did not protest or
launch into a hundred and one reasons why she should
heed him. She wanted to go and she was going to go,
and short of tying her up he could not stop her.

Darting in under the lintel, Nate gasped as a wave of
blistering heat slammed into him, nearly driving him
back against Winona. More wood had been used in the
construction of the temple than in the apartments, a lot
more wood, and now that wood crackled the temple's
death knell. The roar of fire on the higher levels was like
the whoosh of wind on a blustery day.

A short passageway led to an expansive chamber. Far
overhead beams were ablaze, raining cinders and sparks
onto the ornately decorated floor. A section of the opposite wall had fallen, showering a massive amount of
stone and mortar and wood onto a group of priests
and others. Their crushed, ravaged bodies lay amid the
rubble.

Nate counted three passages at the north and south
ends of the chamber. The place was a maze of corridors
and rooms that would take months to explore fully, and
he had mere minutes to find Nevava before the whole
roof came crashing down. As he debated which passage
to take, it dawned on him that he might not recognize
the boy even if he saw him, not if the Anasazis had
dressed him in Anasazis garb and cut his hair to match
theirs.

Winona saw two women emerge from a hall, coughing
and sputtering, their hands over their mouths. Smoke had

gotten into their eyes, which were watering profusely, and they stumbled as if drunk, groping toward the passage that would take them to the main entrance.

"Let's try that one!" Nate said, picking a hall on the right at random. Dodging cinders and debris, he sprinted toward it. A hiss overhead alerted him to a falling piece of wood as long as his arm. He leaped out of harm's way with a whisker to spare.

"That was too close for comfort," Nate remarked. Winona did not respond as he threaded a course toward the corridor, passing a prone man who wore a mask that resembled a bird's head, and feathers in imitation of plumage. Nate recognized that mask and drew up short.

Evidently Wakonhomin had been heading for the entrance when a portion of the roof weighing several hundred pounds smashed onto him. The High Priest's torso and hips had been flattened to a grisly pulp. Only his bizarre mask and feathered arms and legs were showing.

Nate was wasting precious moments. "Hurry," he said, vaulting over a beam. The south side of the temple had sustained the most damage from the quake. Mounds of litter were as abundant as sand dunes in a desert. He weaved among them until he came to a clear space.

Ahead was the corridor, mired in shadow. Nate was a few strides from the opening when he saw the giant slab that blocked it, just inside. From under the slab jutted a hand. "Damn!" He bent his shoulder to the obstacle and pushed for all he was worth, but it was like trying to move a mountain.

"Forget this one." Nate turned toward the passageway on their left, when suddenly it hit him that his wife had not said a word since they entered the great chamber. "Winona?" he said, pivoting, and was stunned to his core to find he was alone. "It just can't be!" he blurted, taking a step. But it was.

Winona had disappeared.

135

Chapter Fifteen

Minutes earlier, when Winona King saw the two women groping blindly for the way out of the temple, she had rushed over and taken the foremost by the hand. From the Anasazi's eyes streamed a torrent of tears. When Winona gripped her and pulled her toward the right passageway, the woman mumbled a few words, possibly in gratitude.

Winona, not responding, hastened the pair along. She was anxious to rejoin her husband, who was heading toward the south end of the huge chamber, unaware of what she had done. Winona would have called out to let him know, but that would announce to all the fleeing Anasazis in the chamber that she was not one of them. No sense in inviting trouble, she mused.

A logjam had formed at the entrance to the corridor that linked the chamber to the plaza. More than a dozen Anasazi men and women were all trying to get through the opening simultaneously, with predictable results.

Most, like the women Winona guided, had been blinded by the stinging smoke and were half out of their minds with fear.

Winona owed the Anasazis nothing. To them she was an enemy to be enslaved or slain. Yet she could not bring herself to run off after Nate knowing that some or all of them would perish if they did not escape the building before the roof came crashing down.

So without hesitation Winona barreled into the thick of the melee and sought to restore some semblance of order. Not being able to communicate handicapped her immensely. She had to resort to pushing and pulling and barring the way of some of the more frantic ones so that others could slip into the corridor without hindrance.

Three or four were able to untangle themselves and do so. Winona pried two women apart who were battling to see who would go next, and held on to the more frantic of the pair so the other one could dart to safety.

The frantic one was outraged by Winona's interference and began to berate her in the Anasazi tongue. Suddenly the woman's eyes widened. She had gotten a good look at Winona and realized Winona was not one of them. Yelling shrilly, she abruptly stopped trying to break free and instead tried to seize Winona.

A number of other Anasazis paused in their headlong flight to turn and stare. They saw an outsider in their midst, an outsider who had no business being there. Worse, an outsider who mysteriously appeared at the very moment their city was stricken by calamity. Some immediately jumped to the conclusion that there must be a connection, that the outsider was bad medicine and had somehow brought the disaster down on them. Others unconsciously channeled the impotent fury they felt because they were unable to do anything about the spreading destruction toward this outsider. Here was someone they could vent their fury on, and vent it they did.

Winona sensed the rising tide of hatred and pivoted to dash into the open. She took but a stride when they were on her, seven, eight, nine of them, men and women alike, yowling like rabid coyotes and battering her with fists and open hands. Under the human deluge she went down to her knees, and lost her rifle.

Raising her arms overhead to ward off the worst of the blows, Winona levered herself erect and fought to get clear. She hit, she pushed, she kicked, but they had her hemmed in now, ten or eleven of them, their faces contorted by hatred so potent that it transformed them from human beings into demons, into a bloodthirsty bestial pack that would not be satisfied with anything short of her death.

Winona opened her mouth to shout for Nate and was struck on the jaw by a heavy fist. Stunned, she sagged onto her left knee. It was the moment the Anasazis awaited. Screaming and raving, they closed in, battering her mercilessly.

She tried to protect herself, but there was only so much she could do. Tucking into a ball, she let her back and shoulders absorb the worst of it. One factor in her favor was that the Anasazis were so tightly packed together they were hampering one another; they actually fought among themselves for the right to beat her to death.

Winona saw an opening between a pair of legs and shot through it like a prairie dog down its burrow. Momentarily free, she scrambled to her feet. Or tried to. A tremendous blow between her shoulder blades drove her to her knees again, and before she could recover the Anasazis were on her, hammering her head and neck and body.

A sob escaped Winona's lips, a sob of frustration. She had only been trying to help the Anasazis, and *this* was how they repaid her! She sobbed, too, at the thought of dying so far from her home and her people, and at the idea of never seeing her husband or her children again.

A jarring kick to the ribs whooshed the air from Winona's lungs and lanced her with mind-searing agony so acute the world around her spun. Dizzy, nauseous, she marshaled her strength and began to fight back.

Shoshones did not go meekly to their deaths. Warriors or maidens, it made no difference. They were not cowards, and they clung tenaciously to life for as long as it animated their limbs.

Winona pushed a woman so hard, the woman went sprawling. Heaving into a crouch, she rammed her shoulder into the big belly of a priest trying to bash in her skull. A warrior gripped her from behind, his arm encircling her waist. As he lifted her, exposing her to the blows of the others, she whipped her head back, into his nose. She heard a loud crunch, and the warrior roared like a wounded bear.

But he did not let her go. Winona stamped her foot onto his instep. His grip slackened, though not enough, so she did it again and again, heedless of the knuckles that thudded into her chest and sides and the ringing slap of a palm on her cheek and the sting of nails raking her neck.

The Anasazis were beside themselves. Screeching, bawling, howling, they shouldered one another aside for the right to strike her next. Gone was any semblance of rational thought. They were a mindless mass bent on murderous intent. They were not people, they were not animals. They were worse than animals. Any shred of intelligence had fled, replaced by raw savagery.

Against that irresistible tide of primitive blood lust, what chance did Winona have? The warrior heaved her into their midst, and they were on her like ravenous wolves on a doe. She landed a punch or two, but for each one of hers that connected she was in turn pummeled a score of times.

Winona's strength was ebbing. In desperation she clawed for her knife and succeeded in grabbing the hilt. She cut into a man about to batter her with both his hands locked together, then slashed a woman trying to claw out her eyes.

The Anasazis gave way. Encouraged, Winona swung wildly to keep the pack at bay. Those in front of her backed off, but those behind her pounced. Iron fingers found her knife arm and clamped it in a vise. She sobbed again as the ones in front renewed their attack. Her knife was torn from her grasp.

The next moment, Winona was on the floor. A ring of distorted snarling visages swooped down on her and the pain became worse than ever, much, much worse. She felt darkness nipping at her mind, and she tenderly voiced the word that meant the most to her in all the world: "Nate!"

"Did you hear something?"

Zach King was seated on the lip of a slope, the Hawken across his thighs. Behind him were the hobbled horses, including the pony. The stupid cayuse had nearly gotten him killed once; it wouldn't get the chance to do so again.

On hearing his sister's question, Zach shifted and surveyed the terraces above. Other than the sigh of the wind, which had picked up in the past fifteen minutes, he heard nothing unusual. "No. Why?"

Evelyn was not entirely sure. She would be the first to admit her nerves were shot. The ordeal in the forest had left her as jumpy as a rabbit that had caught the scent of a fox. Every little noise she could not account for was made by a monster creeping toward them.

She had tried to tell herself that it was all in her head. That maybe the things they had seen were not monsters after all, but animals they mistook for monsters. The brute that had chased them might well have been a bear, its features twisted by the play of starlight and shadows. Those red wolves that roamed the valley were just that— reddish wolves. Nothing peculiar there, since wolves came in a variety of colors. She had personally seen gray wolves and black wolves and even a few white wolves. As for the giant lizard that killed the Utes, sure, it was bigger than any lizard she ever heard of. But by the same token, her own pa had once tangled with a grizzly twice the size of most silvertips. And the Shoshones, among other tribes, believed in the existence of something called the Thunder Bird, a hawklike bird bigger than a horse. So an overgrown lizard was not all that extraordinary.

Still, Evelyn could not help jumping every time she heard a sound from above. A howl, a squeal, they were all the same, all fraught with menace.

Now she stiffened and turned on hearing an odd swishing noise, sort of like the noise she would make walking through a field of tall grass. The slopes above were empty of life, so it had to be her imagination.

Zach saw his sister scan the upper terraces, and did likewise. He knew she was terrified, and he considered scolding her for being so childish. But after their harrowing trial in the woods, he figured he would go easy on her. "You're hearing things, sis," he said, and went to resume his scrutiny of the valley floor and the road leading to the Anasazi city.

A faint swish was his first inkling that maybe Evelyn's ears were not deceiving her. Zach scoured the high terraces a second time, more intently than before, and the short hairs at the nape of his neck prickled when he detected movement where there should be none, movement so startling and horrifying that for a few shocked seconds he gaped, dumbstruck.

A sinuous shadow was winding downward, a shadow so broad and so long that Zach could be forgiven for not recognizing it for what it was right away. The shape was low to the ground, so low that its blunt head cleaved the grass like the prow of a ship cleaving the sea. In sinuous S-shaped movements the colossal thing-that-should-not-be glided slowly toward them.

"It's a snake!" Zach breathed, and was on his feet in a flash. Springing to the horses, he worked frantically to remove their hobbles, saying over a shoulder, "Help me, or we'll be eaten alive!"

Evelyn wanted to help. She honestly and truly did. But her legs were paralyzed by fright so potent it chilled her soul. As she had done with the wolves and the lizard, she tried to convince herself it was just a snake, just an awfully big snake the night made seem even bigger. *Just a snake! Just a snake! Just a snake!* she mentally chanted. But it was useless. She could not deny her own eyes. Yes, it was a snake, but it was much more. It was exactly like the giant serpents her mother had told her about. Maybe it was one of them.

"Sis!" Zach barked harshly when Evelyn did not budge. He could not do it all himself, not in time to get out of there before the snake reached them. Finishing with the bay, he turned to his father's stallion.

George Washington nickered, and the whinny broke the spell that held Evelyn in place. Her pony, her friend, was in danger. She tore at his hobbles, shutting her mind to the thing above them, refusing to think about it for fear she would freeze again.

The swishing grew louder, punctuated by a sibilant hiss. Zach glanced up and beheld a sight that would petrify grown men.

The snake had paused and reared, its triangular head swaying from side to side as it regarded the horses and humans through orbs that gleamed with yellow fire. Still forty yards away, it appeared to be almost on top of them.

A forked tongue flicked in and out, stabbing the air for their scent.

Zach moved to his mother's mare. He never even considered using his rifle. Snakes had few vital organs; at that range, in the dark, with a serpent that size, he would be kidding himself if he thought he could bring it down with one shot. Or two. Or three.

"I'm done!" Evelyn announced, popping erect. Something—the sound of her voice, her movement—caused the snake to flatten and crawl swiftly forward. She clutched at the pony's reins but missed. "Zach!" she wailed, spiked by panic.

Meanwhile, the serpent bore down on them like a living nightmare.

In a berserk rage Nate King plowed into the Anasazis who surrounded his wife. He had seen her go down as he rushed across the chamber to her rescue, and when he reached the Anasazis it was not Nathaniel King, meek New York accountant, who tore into them, or Nate King, hardy free trapper. It was someone else entirely, a throwback to the trace of Nordic blood in his veins. It was a barbarian, a Crusader, a Viking all rolled into one. It was elemental man, savage man, man protecting the woman he held dearest of all.

He did not act according to reason, because reason had fled. He did not think and then act, because conscious thought was gone. Raw instinct thrust him into the thick of the Anasazis. Instinct, and pure ferocity.

Nate had picked up part of a broken beam. A yard long and as thick around as his thigh at one end, it made for a stout club. Flailing it right and left, he rained blows on the Anasazis, felling four of them before the remainder awakened to his presence. The heavy thuds of his club were drowned out by their oaths and cries.

They surged against him like surf pounding on breakers, seeking to overpower him by sheer weight of numbers. For a moment they almost succeeded. Warriors had him by the legs and one arm, and a woman clung to his chest, impeding him. His legs started to buckle under the strain, causing the Anasazis to whoop in triumph.

They were premature. Nate King planted both feet firmly and refused to go down, even if every last one piled on top of him. With a mighty shake of his chest, he dislodged the woman, freeing his arms so he could attack the warriors holding his legs. One collapsed with a split head; the other sustained a broken arm.

Heaving upright, Nate laid about him with a vengeance, his club connecting with each swing. He felled Anasazis right and left, felled them as they hit and stabbed and clawed, felled them as they circled and leaped and dived, felled them as more poured from a side tunnel to join the unequal clash.

Broken women and men littered the floor, groaning, spitting blood, convulsing.

A warrior with a lance appeared and flung it, wooden lightning that impaled a woman who blundered in front of the mountain man at the wrong moment.

A woman holding a knife tried to plunge it into Nate's groin and was rewarded with a broken shoulder.

Nate swung in a frenzy, never picking targets but striking as they presented themselves. He did not know how many Anasazis he had downed, or how many more there were. He swung until he realized his makeshift club beat empty air.

A red haze seemed to lift from Nate's eyes. He saw bodies on all sides, bodies he had shattered, some never to rise again. As he lowered his arms, the huge roof rumbled, a portent of its imminent collapse.

"Winona!" Nate cried, and spun, seeking the love of his life. She lay where she had fallen, pale as a ghost, her dress stained scarlet. "Winona?" he repeated, but she did not respond. She did not even move.

Chapter Sixteen

It would have been so easy for Zachary King to vault onto his bay and race down the terraces well head of the slithering horror that drew nearer every instant. But to do so he must abandon his sister, a notion he never entertained. As many spats as they'd had, as many times as he had wanted to throttle her, he could no more desert her than he could stop breathing. Taking a bound, he forked his hands under her arms, swept her onto the pony, and hollered, "Ride, sis! Ride like the wind!"

Most girls would have done so. Most would have spurred their mounts over the crest without looking back. Evelyn was different. She was much too young to realize it, but she was made of sterner stuff. She had what her pa would call "true grit." "I'm not going without you," she responded.

Zach did not dispute the point. The snake was only twenty yards away, gliding swiftly along, quicksilver with scales. Snatching the reins to the stallion and the mare, he leaped onto his bay and lit out of there as if his britches were ablaze. "Dally and we're dead!"

Evelyn was not about to. A jab of her heels sent the spooked pony over the rim. George Washington seemed to know what was at stake, for he flew like the winged horse Pegasus in a tale her father had read to her one evening before bedtime. It was all she could do to hold on. Mane and tail flying, George Washington proved that the size of a horse was no indication of how fast it could go. Most horses were larger than he was, but few could have flown faster down those slopes.

The pony went so fast, in fact, that Evelyn feared for their safety. A misstep was all it would take. In the dark she could not see ruts and holes. Should George Washington step into one they both would go down, George Washington with a broken leg, she to fall prey to the massive reptile that wanted them for supper. Automatically, she slowed a trifle.

"What in the world are you doing?" Zach demanded. He was right behind her, hauling on the reins to the other horses. Shifting, he saw the serpent hurtling on their heels, now fifteen yards off and closing rapidly.

The road was their only hope, Zach reckoned. On a flat, straight stretch the horses could outrun the snake. The trick lay in reaching the road alive. It seemed impossibly far away, a pale ribbon in the vast darkness of the night, so near and yet so distant.

"It's gaining!" Evelyn cried, and imagined being swallowed whole. A sickening feeling came over her. Her stomach churned. She imagined what it would be like to slide down the snake's gullet, to have its digestive juices get into her nose, her eyes, her mouth. To have her skin eaten away and the breath stolen from her body.

"Go! Go!" Zach hollered when the pony began to flag. He was prepared to let go of the stallion and the mare and pluck her from her saddle, if the need arose.

The Lost Valley

She was more important than any old horse. Heck, she was more important than all the horses put together.

The pale ribbon widened. It was so tantalizingly close that Zach had the illusion he could reach out and touch it, but the truth was that several terraces stood between them and their salvation. He urged the bay to greater speed and pulled alongside George Washington. His sister was clinging to the pony like a drowning woman would cling to a log. She smiled gamely at him, and he had never loved her more than that exact moment.

"We're almost there!"

The thunder of hoofs was as nothing compared to the earlier thunder of the earthquake, but it was sufficiently loud to echo off the high cliffs and make it seem as if a herd of buffalo were stampeding.

Ahead lay the last terrace. Zach spurred the bay into putting on an extra burst of speed. Evelyn was only a few feet behind him as they clattered onto the dirt road and reined toward the city. "Don't stop for nothing!"

Evelyn was not about to. She didn't care if a horde of Anasazi warriors were to rise up in front of them; she would not slow down. Let them deal with the snake. If they dared.

Zach looked back to see how much of a lead they had. It should be about ten yards, but it wasn't. Stupefied, he scanned the lowest terrace, then the one above it, concentrating on the areas deepest in shadow. The serpent had to be there, somewhere, yet for the life of him he couldn't find it.

Galloping another hundred feet, Zach drew rein and called out for his sister to do the same. As the bay came to a halt he turned his mount broadside so he could plainly see the road and the benighted slopes.

Evelyn thought he was loco, but she did as he bid her. On studying the tilled terraces she exclaimed in consternation, "Where did it get to? It was there a moment ago."

Corn rattled in the breeze. Row after row of carefully cultivated vegetables stretched to the north and the south in undisturbed ranks. On the upper terraces not a living creature was visible. The giant snake had disappeared off the face of the earth.

Zach checked the other side of the road in case the serpent had crossed when they weren't looking. As startled as he was by the absence of the reptile, he was even more shocked to see the lake had also vanished. For a body of water that size to simply blink out of existence defied belief. Yet he knew he had seen it earlier. As for the snake, could it be they had imagined the whole thing?

Evelyn did not like sitting there. The scaly horror had to be nearby, probably slinking toward them unseen, ready to rear and strike when their guard was down. "What are we waiting for?" she asked impatiently.

"Nothing," Zach admitted, and trotted on. Now that they were safe, he had another problem to deal with. Namely, what should they do next? Anasazis were bound to be abroad, and who knew what else? They needed a hiding place, a place where they could watch the road for their mother and father. But precious few trees grew on the valley floor, and fewer tracts of undergrowth.

"Look yonder," Evelyn said. "Their city is burning."

That it was. Flames leaped from many a rooftop, licked at many a wall. Zach recollected his pa reading to him about a place called Pompeii and idly wondered if the scene he beheld was similar to the fabled city's last moments.

Evelyn bit her lower lip in heartfelt dismay. Her folks were in that terrible place, beset by the heat and the smoke. Screams wafted to her, screams and the hubbub of hurting, scared people. The Anasazis must be beside themselves, and in that state they might do anything to her mother and father.

Zach was likewise glued to the spectacle. He did not pay particular attention to the road ahead. A snort by the bay remedied his mistake, but too late. Directly under its front legs yawned a chasm where none should be.

Flinging the beam to the floor, Nate King ran to his wife and knelt. ''Winona?'' he cried, his voice quavering from the emotion that clawed at his insides like the razor talons of a bird of prey. He could not bear to think of losing her, not her, not the kindest, most loving woman he had ever met, not the woman who cherished him with all her heart, the woman who had given him the greatest gift any woman could ever give a man: her undying love.

More and more smoke cascaded from on high as Nate gently lifted his wife's head onto his lap. He felt her neck for a pulse and did not find one. Despair swamped him. He went dead inside, as if someone had thrown a switch and all sensation had fled his body. Sagging over her, his finger moved a quarter of an inch. Suddenly a bolt of lightning jolted him. He had probed the wrong spot! She did have a pulse, a strong steady heartbeat, and as tears of supreme joy moistened his eyes, she opened hers.

''You saved me.''

It was a simple statement, yet the tone she used expressed the depth of her love as eloquently as a poem.

''The next time you take it into that pretty head of yours to go up against an entire tribe by yourself, remember what I always do when I'm outnumbered.''

''Which is?''

''I run.''

Winona smiled, and regretted it when her puffy lower lip flared with torment. Casting her arms around him, she held him close and would not let go. Not even when the roof rumbled and burning embers showered around them.

It was when the floor rumbled and shook that Nate lifted his head and saw the walls sway and the burning beams above them jiggle dangerously. "Another quake," he warned Winona, pulling her upright. "An aftershock, they call it." As he said it, the rumbling ceased.

Winona had to lean against him for support. Her legs were weak, her muscles were like mush, a delayed reaction to the punishment she had suffered. She felt sore all over, from the crown of her head to the tips of her toes. Her back and shoulders had borne the brunt of the blows and hurt viciously when she moved.

"Can you walk?" Nate asked. The roof was perilously close to collapse, and he did not want to be under it when the tons of fiery debris fell.

"I can if you need me to." Gritting her teeth, Winona straightened unaided and moved stiffly to her rifle. As she bent, her lower back knotted in a spasm and she inadvertently uttered a low cry.

"Let me," Nate said, retrieving the Hawken himself. Looking at her tore his heart. Her left eye was swollen half shut, both cheeks had been raked and clawed, her neck was bloody, her mouth would take weeks to heal. And those were just the visible wounds. He shuddered to think how many welts and bruises must cover her body.

"Where to, husband?" Winona asked, full well knowing his answer.

"We still have to find the boy."

"I will be right behind you." Winona mustered a wan grin. "And this time, I will stay behind you."

Nate clasped her wrist and steered her to a passage on the left. It was dark, narrow, foreboding, as still as a crypt. Most of the Anasazis who had been inside when the destruction occurred were either gone or had perished. Quite probably the Ute boy had also fled or was lying dead somewhere in the temple. But Nate could not just up and leave, not without trying to find out.

A large crack had split the right-hand wall. Another, farther on, ran the width of the ceiling. Thinner ones were more common the farther they went, and around a wide bend they came on a partially crumbled section.

Nate began to worry that another aftershock might bring the whole passageway toppling down. They passed doorways, some to small rooms, others to spacious chambers. Here and there they came on lifeless Anasazis, most crushed by falling slabs.

The smoke grew steadily thicker, to the point that Nate found it difficult to breathe. He had about made up his mind that he had done all he could and it would be better to seek an avenue of escape when yet another room appeared on the left. In it were war clubs, lances, and knives, enough to outfit an army. Since these were of no special interest to him, he was almost past it when he glanced into a far corner.

"My guns!"

Not only his rifle and flintlocks, but his knife and tomahawk, his possibles bag, and his ammo pouch were all there. In short order he was armed to the teeth and feeling fit to tussle with a ravening griz.

"I have not seen you this happy since you traded for your stallion," Winona mentioned lightheartedly. Her husband was grinning like a Shoshone boy just given his very first bow. Men were like that, though. At heart they were all oversized boys.

"We must hurry," Nate said, taking her hand once more.

The corridor wound upward to a flight of stairs. A gust of air gave Nate hope they were near one of the side entrances, but the stairs brought them to a balcony of sorts on the north side of the temple. Steps led down to the plaza, where mass confusion continued to reign.

Pausing, Nate faced the passage. Dared he risk another try at finding Nevava? As if in answer, from the bowels of the temple came a thunderous boom and seconds later a gusting cloud of dust and heat spewed over them, compelling Nate to cover his face with a hand.

Far down the corridor a pinpoint of light sparkled, a pinpoint that expanded and swelled until it filled the entire passageway even as it spurted toward the balcony at twice the speed a man could run. "Look out!" Nate hollered, throwing himself against Winona and sweeping her to the side.

From out of the corridor belched searing flames that lapped at the dark like so many tongues. Briefly, a good portion of the plaza was lit up as bright as day, revealing scores of dead and dying, countless dazed and wounded, and the few who were trying in vain to stem the tide of disaster.

Intense heat ballooned around the Kings, transforming the balcony into a furnace. Heat so hot it threatened to incinerate their clothes and sear them to the bone. Nate shielded Winona, feeling as if he were being fried alive. His back, the back of his legs, the nape of his neck, they were as hot as molten lava. Or so it seemed.

As quickly as the flames flared, they died. With an arm around Winona's waist, Nate hustled down the steps, relishing the cool breeze that had sprung up. At the bottom he nearly tripped over a priest whose head resembled a squashed pumpkin thanks to a bloody chunk of roof.

"Where to now? Winona asked.

Nate's first inclination was to keep on searching, but the pain in her voice, the misery etched on her face, stirred him into saying, "We're getting the hell out of here."

"Are you sure that is best?"

"I'm sure."

Holding her close, Nate moved away from the steps. Enough smoke blanketed the plaza that they should be able to make it across if they avoided clusters of Anasazis. "Ready to do some running?"

"Whatever must be done, I will do."

Nate could never say what made him glance back. He had no intimation that anyone was behind them. No noise or movement demanded investigation. He just looked over his shoulder and there, under the steps, deep in shadow, was a small huddled form. Something inside of him spurred him to go see what it was.

Winona raised her head when her man turned. She saw a child of ten or so, a boy clad in buckskin leggings with his thin arms around his bent knees, a terrified child whose wide eyes were damp with tears. "Nevava?"

The Ute boy blinked, then wiped at his eyes. "Who are you? I have never seen you before."

Nate had learned enough of the Ute tongue to get by, enough to reply, "We are friends of Red Feather. We are here to take you back to your people."

Nevava shot to his feet, his fear forgotten. "You knew my father?"

"I met him—" Nate began, and was cut short by nearly having his legs jarred out from under him by another quake. An aftershock, he thought. But unlike the last one, it grew more and more violent until it rivaled the quake that had destroyed the city, then surpassed it. The ground bucked and shook and pitched him to his knees. He heard Nevava cry out, and raised his head.

The upper third of the north wall had split nearly in half and was teetering outward, poised to snuff out their lives.

Chapter Seventeen

Zach King hauled on the bay's reins harder than he had ever pulled on a pair of reins in his whole life, harder than any rider ever should, so hard that the animal's mouth would be sore for a week. And as he did, he slammed his legs against its sides.

Horses were unpredictable at times. In moments of stress they did not always do as their riders desired. The bay was a case in point.

Zach intended to wheel it to the right to avoid the yawning crevice, but instead the bay bounded to the left, hopping stiff-legged like a giant rabbit. It cleared the edge of the crevice with barely a hand's width to spare, while the stallion and the mare cleared it by a wider margin. Zach trotted a dozen yards before he brought them to a halt.

As for Evelyn, her pony shied wide of the cavity, allowing her to avoid it with no problem. But now she was on one side of the rift, her brother on the other.

154

The Lost Valley

Annoyed that the bay had not done as he wanted, Zach raised a hand to give it a smack, then changed his mind. Now that he thought about it, he realized the horse had been smarter than he was. If it had veered to the right as he wanted, it would have collided with George Washington and maybe sent him over the brink into the fissure. While Zach would not miss the pony one little bit, his sister was another story.

"Zach, how do we get back together?" she called out.

The crevice was only six feet across at the widest, but Zach did not have a hankering to jump it, not in the dark, not when he could not see the bottom even when he rose in the stirrups and leaned way out over the chasm. "Keep going. It might narrow farther along."

It did, another forty yards on. Evelyn was glad to be reunited, even though she did not admit as much. Her brother had a habit of poking fun at her when she showed too much affection. Why that should be had puzzled her for the longest while. Her mother always showed tremendous affection for her father and her pa did not mind. But she had to take into account that her pa was a man, and boys were different from men. They had worse table manners, for one thing.

She was reminded of what her uncle Shakespeare had once said when a boy at a rendezvous had taken to pulling her hair. "Always try to remember, princess, that a little girl is a little lady waiting to sprout, while a little boy is a pint-sized hellion." She had understood that part, but then Shakespeare added, "And may never the twain meet until they're old enough to know better." Whatever that meant.

"So now what?" Evelyn asked after they had ridden a spell in nervous silence.

Zach was glad she could not read the indecision in his eyes. She was relying on him to pull them through, to keep them safe until they rejoined their parents. The trou-

155

ble was, he was at a loss. They needed to hide. But where? There was no cover within a quarter of a mile—or was there?

Ahead lay a terrace seeded with corn. The stalks were not fully grown, but they were high enough to suit him.

"Follow me," Zach said.

They had to climb a short tract of open slope to reach the crop. Zach was in the lead, tugging on the reins to the mare and the stallion, when without warning both horses whinnied and tried to break loose. His own bay snorted, then plunged, almost throwing him.

"Zach!" Evelyn shouted, goading her pony forward to help. Suddenly George Washington began to twist and fight the bit, and she had her hands full keeping him under control.

A low rumbling resounded in all directions, swelling in volume, steadily swelling until the entire valley reverberated like one gigantic drum. And as the sound swelled, the ground under them shook with more and more force until the horses were slipping and tilting and stayed upright only by a monumental effort.

This time Evelyn was not afraid. She knew what she was dealing with, and that she was safe as long as George Washington did not fall on her. Then she recalled the wide fissure in the road, a fissure where she was sure there had not been one before the sun went down. She put two and two together and leaped to the conclusion that the earthquake was to blame, that it could split the earth as easily as she split a loaf of bread. And if it should do that underneath her, she would be gobbled whole like a ripe berry.

The quake did not last long. Zach managed to hold on to the extra horses, and once assured his sister was all right, he made his way to the rows of corn. They dismounted, used a rope taken from one of his father's parfleches to tether the four mounts, and sat side by side, their elbows nearly touching.

"I plumb forgot those hobbles," Zach remarked. "Hope Pa doesn't bend my ear for being forgetful again."

"I'll stick up for you," Evelyn said. "But I wouldn't worry. If you'd taken the time to grab them, that snake would have grabbed you. Pa would rather have you than a bunch of hobbles any old day."

"We're pretty lucky to have them for parents, aren't we?" Zach said. He had never really given it much thought before, tending to take his ma and pa for granted. But they were always there for his sister and him, always looking out for their welfare.

"I'd say so." Evelyn had always rated her mother as the best mother in all creation. When she came down sick, her mother mended her. When she wanted a new dress or some such, her mother always made it or helped her get it. When she had wanted a horse of her own, it had been her mother who talked her father into going to Bent's Fort and bartering for George Washington. Yes, a mother was a girl's best friend.

Time passed, anxious time spent worrying. Evelyn grew drowsy and had to shake her head often to stay awake. Her lids had closed for the fiftieth time when she was startled to feel the grass under her rise up as if to pitch her headlong down the slope.

"Another quake," Zach cried, leaping to the horses. "Grab that mangy critter of yours."

Scrambling to her feet, Evelyn lurched toward her pony. The unstable footing threw her off stride, and she tottered as some of the trappers did when they had too much liquor. Snatching George Washington's reins, she sought to calm him, but he pranced wildly and it was all she could do to hold on.

Zach figured this latest quake would be like the

last, short and mild, but he was woefully mistaken. It was the most violent yet, and it seemed to go on and on and on. How he held on to the three horses he would never know. Presently the shaking tapered to mild tremors, and he congratulated himself on having lived through it without anything going wrong.

At that very instant the stallion reared, tearing from his grasp. Still holding on to the mare and the bay, he ran after the big black as it cantered onto the road and stopped, its ears pricked.

"Dang it," Zach complained, sliding on the slick grass. He spread his legs to brace himself, but his left foot snagged on a bump and down he went, sprawling onto the road on his hands and knees. His only consolation was that the stallion had not gone any farther.

"I always reckoned Pa trained you better," Zach told it as he placed the stock of his rifle on the ground and used it to pump himself up out of the dirt.

"Say! What's that?" Evelyn hollered.

Zach looked where she was pointing. To the south inky figures moved, flowing toward them. Or rather, toward him, for the figures were coming down the center of the road. He did not need the starlight to identify the onrushing forms. Apprehension seized him by the throat as his mind screamed, *Anasazis!*

Some men and women are gifted with superior reflexes. They can run faster, throw farther, jump higher. They are the physical cream of the crop, the ones who make exceptional athletes. In ancient times it was such as these who gained immortal fame in the Olympic Games.

Nate King had never participated in a sporting event in his life, but if he had it was likely he'd have won a few. For even among the mountain men, who were as tough a breed as ever lived, he was one of the fastest, the strongest, the most agile.

He gave the wilderness the credit. The constant grueling fight for survival had tempered the soft sinews of a New York accountant into muscles of virtual steel.

Everyday tasks around the cabin likewise hardened a man. There was wood to be chopped, horses to be shod, game for the supper pot to hunt, and a thousand and one other jobs that kept a man busy from dawn until well past dusk.

As a result, Nate King was in his physical prime. He had an iron frame, lightning reflexes, and they were both put to the ultimate test by what happened next.

With a rending roar the massive section of all three floors above them plummeted groundward. Nate bent, wrapped his left arm around the Ute boy, whirled, and ran. His wife had turned to flee, but she was in no condition to sprint. The brutal beating had taken a fearful toll. She was slow, much too slow.

Nate scooped Winona into his right arm, lifting her clear off her feet. He pumped his legs, barely feeling the strain of bearing both his wife and the boy and both rifles. A quick tilt of his head showed the wall swooping down on them. It loomed blackly against the backdrop of flames consuming the temple, blotting out the sky.

Streaking toward the plaza, Nate heard Nevava gasp in fear and the boy went as rigid as a board. A shadow fell across them, a shadow that grew larger and larger and darker and darker. Nate could sense how close the falling wall was. Intuition told him that in the next several heartbeats it would smash onto them with pulverizing force.

Winona held herself limp to make it easier for Nate. She did not look up; she did not want to know how close the end was. Her confidence in her husband was unbounded, but she was a practical person and she knew the odds were against them. For Nate to be able to out-race the slab while carrying both of them was next to impossible.

She thought of Evelyn and Zach, her precious children, the two who had given her so much joy, who had made her laugh and on occasion brought tears to her eyes. She would have liked to see them grow up, to see Evelyn wed and Zach grow into a respected warrior. She would have liked to bounce their children on her knee, to be called "grandmother" and to see a whole new generation blossom.

Winona blinked, and saw the dark shadow blot out all the light. The slab was almost upon them. The remainder of her life could be measured in fractions of a moment.

Nate King realized the same thing. Taking one more mighty bound, he flung himself outward, his steel-spring legs hurtling the three of them through the air as if they had been hurled from a catapult. Six, eight feet he leaped, and as he came down he twisted so his shoulder bore the impact. At the instant of contact Nate rolled, not once but over and over in a whirlwind of motion.

Behind them a thunderous blast rocked the plaza. Under them the ground shook as if from another quake. Around them and on top of them rained stones and mortar, some pieces small but others large, pelting them, stinging them, bruising them.

Their momentum expended, they came to a stop. Nate was on the bottom, on his back, and raising his head, he saw a mountain of debris where the slab had hit. It had missed them by six inches, if that much.

"You did it," Winona said softly. Tenderly, she pressed her sore lips to his cheek.

Nevava was trembling like an aspen leaf in a strong wind. Nate set the boy down and stiffly sat up. Somehow he had managed to hold on to the rifles, and he gave Winona hers. "As much as I'd like to sit here awhile, we can't,'' he said. In the Ute tongue, he asked the boy, "Can you stand?"

Nevava rose unsteadily. He was scared and shaken, but like a true warrior's son he was doing his best to hide it.

Half of the temple had been devoured by the fire. In its flickering glow much of the plaza and the surrounding apartments were starkly revealed, showing the extensive damage wrought by the latest quake. Weakened by the earlier tremors, the walls and roofs had folded like a house of cards, collapsing in on top one another in a domino effect, starting with the highest levels and proceeding down to the lowest.

More dwellings had been destroyed than were left standing. Jagged remnants of walls and isolated beams thrust skyward like tombstones in a graveyard. From out of the rubble poked random arms and legs and broken shapes that had once been men, women, or children.

Nate had never been the superstitious kind. He was not one of those who carried a rabbit's foot for luck or believed that finding a four-leaf clover was a good omen. He did not read portents in the stars or signs in ordinary random events. They were so much nonsense as far as he was concerned. But even so, he could not help thinking that the terrible devastation that had befallen the Anasazi city was more than mere happenstance. What they could have done to deserve the destruction, though, was beyond him.

"Come," Nate said in Ute, and hurried to the south. Not as many Anasazis were in the plaza as before, and most of those he saw were so severely hurt they were beyond human help. One older man he would never forget. It was a tiller, a wizened oldster whose left leg had been crushed and whose right arm dangled by a strip of flesh. Yet the man was weakly scrabbling across the ground like a wounded crab, smearing a wide red swatch in his wake.

"Where did they all go?" Winona wondered. She had girded herself for another clash, but the few Anasazis still alive were either in no shape to oppose them or were intent on saving their own hides.

The wind was blowing the smoke to the southeast. A gust parted a swirling gray cloud ahead, revealing a long line of refugees who streamed around the northwest corner of the city, fleeing on the road that crossed the valley.

"There's your answer," Nate said. He noticed she was limping and put an arm around her waist, but she pushed his hand away.

"I can hold my own, husband."

"You and your darned pride."

"Pride has nothing to do with it. You must keep your hands free in case we are attacked. We are not safe yet."

Not by a long shot, Nate mentally agreed. He prayed their kids were all right, that they had stayed where they were supposed to. As he approached the apartment where the Anasazis had imprisoned him, he looked up, thinking of Pedro Valdez and the promise he had made. What would Winona say when she learned they were bound for Texas after they took Nevava to his people? Maybe it would be best if he went himself.

A shriek snapped Nate out of his musing.

Rushing toward them was a bloody apparition, an Anasazi warrior whose right side bore a shallow wound and whose muscular physique was caked with grime and soot. It was Crooked Nose, war club overhead, a knife in his other hand, the gleam of blood lust in his dark eyes.

Winona started to level her rifle, but Nate stepped in front of her. "No. There might be others nearby. Protect the boy. I'll deal with him." And with that, Nate shoved his Hawken into her hand, drew his tomahawk and his knife, and closed on his nemesis.

Chapter Eighteen

There were times when Winona King did not understand her husband at all.

More than sixteen years of marriage had given her keen insight into why he did the things he did. She knew all of his habits and quirks, his likes and dislikes. She knew he liked to sleep on his right side, that he was partial to blackberries above all other foods. She knew his favorite color, which books he liked best, how he felt about the Great Mystery and life in the higher realms.

In short, she knew everything there was to know about the man. So nine times out of ten she could predict how he would react in any given situation. But there was always that tenth time when he behaved exactly the opposite as he should. Such as now.

When the enraged Anasazi charged, Winona fully expected her husband to shoot him. That is what she would have done, what any Shoshone warrior would have done. The Anasazi wanted to kill them, so they should kill him.

Swiftly, efficiently, showing as much mercy as the Anasazi planned to show them.

But not Nate. No, he gave her his rifle and never bothered to draw either flintlock. Instead, he met the Anasazi head-on, using only a knife and tomahawk—in effect meeting the warrior on equal terms.

He was making a mistake. Combat was not a game. Warriors did not play at killing. As her father once instructed her, "There might come a time when our village will be raided, when enemies might try to kill you. Should that happen, remember it is your life or theirs. Do not try to reason with them. They will not listen. Do not try to wound them to spare their lives. You must kill them before they kill you. It is that simple."

It upset Winona no end that her husband had never learned the same lesson. He was forever trying to be "fair," forever striving to do "what was right." He could never bring himself to shoot a foe in the back, or to take undue advantage. Noble sentiments, but exactly the kind of thinking that got a person killed.

So now, as her man and the Anasazi flew at each other, Winona had half a mind to disobey him and shoot the warrior dead. She started to take aim, but she had delayed too long. The moment to act had passed. They were locked in a duel to the death.

Nate countered a swing of the war club with his tomahawk. Shifting, he parried a thrust of Crooked Nose's knife speared at his chest. They circled, trading blows, cold steel ringing on cold steel, war club and tomahawk weaving intricate patterns of skill and trickery.

Crooked Nose feinted, pivoted, snapped his blade at Nate's neck. Deflecting it with his own knife, Nate drove his tomahawk at the Anasazi's midsection, but Crooked Nose was too quick for him.

Borderline madness animated the warrior's features. Crooked Nose fought like someone possessed, with maniacal fury and inhuman strength. Evidently the loss of all he held dear had been more than he could endure.

Nate countered a high slash at his throat, a low cut at his thigh. The swish of their weapons, the crunch of dirt under their feet, their heavy breathing were the only sounds they made. Grim determination compressed their lips, locked their jaws.

From the moment they had set eyes on each other they had been bitter adversaries, and now they vented their shared dislike in a blinding flurry, swinging and spinning and stabbing and hacking too fast for the eye to follow.

They were evenly matched, Nate and the Anasazi. Neither was able to gain the upper hand in the first few moments. Their clash became an endurance test. Which one of them had more stamina? Which one would make the first mistake?

In the ebb and flow of their conflict, it was as if they were joined at the hip. But not in a mutual bond of devotion, as in a marriage. Theirs was a bond of mutual spite. Crooked Nose was the type who hated any who were different from his own kin, and Nate King despised bigots.

Suddenly the Anasazi tucked his knees and flicked the tip of his blade at the mountain man's stomach. Only by a whisker did the trapper deflect the knife.

In retaliation Nate jacked his left knee up, into Crooked Nose's mouth, connecting with an audible crack. Crooked Nose fell backward and Nate warily skipped in to open the other's jugular, but the warrior elevated the war club, foiling him, then sliced the knife at his shin. Nate had to jerk his leg back to spare himself from harm, and in doing so he slipped. His leg was propelled backward while he stumbled forward, directly at the Anasazi.

Crooked Nose flung his arm outward to impale Nate on his blade, but Nate swatted it aside and then brought the tomahawk sizzling downward in a tight arc. Since he was falling as he swung, he could not put all of his weight into the swing and he did not anticipate it being effective.

Fickle fate took a hand. Crooked Nose pumped his war club up to block the tomahawk as he had done a dozen times already. In each instance the club had proven the tomahawk's equal. But this time the short sharp edge of the tomahawk must have caught the club at just the right angle, for it sheared through the wooden club as if it were a piece of kindling, sheared through and thudded into the Anasazi's forehead.

Crooked Nose stiffened and grunted. That was all. His hate-filled eyes locked on Nate, and as he crumbled to the ground he spent the waning seconds of his earthly existence glaring at the object of his hatred.

Nate was breathing hard and caked with sweat. Placing a foot on the warrior's chest, he wrenched the tomahawk out, wiped it clean on the Anasazi's shirt, and slid the handle under his belt. "You had grit, I'll give you that," he said in eulogy.

The smooth feel of a rifle barrel brushing his palm reminded Nate of where he was, and their plight. Accepting the Hawken from his wife, he gestured. "Let's light a shuck while we can."

It was fine by Winona. As no other Anasazis had rushed to aid the warrior, she deduced few were left in the city. The Ute boy hung close to her, like a second shadow, perhaps afraid they would become separated.

Nate jogged from the plaza, pacing himself in order not to tire Winona any more than she already was. They passed more rubble, more bodies. The road was deserted, but to the north spotty wisps of dust confirmed that the general Anasazi population, or, rather, the meager remnants, had forsaken the last of their grand city.

The Kings and Nevava hastened into the night. Winona, recalling her experiences in the forest, remarked, "We must stay alert, husband. There are . . . things . . . in this valley."

"Things? Like the creature that killed this boy's father?"

"That and more."

Just what I need, Nate reflected. Something else to worry about. Zach and Evelyn would be no match for a beast that could slay ten grown men. "Where did you leave the children?"

"It is a ways yet." Winona sensed and shared his anxiety, and hiked faster. Soon the roar of flames dwindled, the infrequent groans and cries faded. She scoured the middle terraces, seeking the exact spot where her son and daughter should be waiting for them. Because she was concentrating on the upper slopes, she was startled when a feminine squeal gushed from a row of corn at the side of the road.

"Ma! Pa!"

Out of the corn darted Evelyn, grinning from ear to ear. She had been fighting sleep, her eyelids drooping, when footfalls stirred her to wakefulness. Now she threw herself into her mother's arms and hugged her mother close, saying repeatedly, "You're alive! You're alive! You're alive!"

Zach emerged, leading all four horses. He was ashamed to admit that he had dozed off, and to cover his embarrassment he said, "For a second there I figured you were more Anasazis. They've been drifting by for the past half an hour."

"Did they give you any trouble?" Nate asked. He had an urge to embrace his son, but did not out of respect for the boy's wishes. A while back Zach had made it plain that he did not like to be fawned over in front of others. "Childish," Zach had called it. The boy would learn better, someday.

167

"None at all, Pa. We were on the road when the first bunch showed up. But they treated us as if we weren't even here. Most were in shock, it looked like."

Nate turned and gazed out over the lost valley of the Anasazis, wondering what the few survivors would do now that the last stronghold of their once flourishing empire had been destroyed. He thought about Pahchatka and hoped the man was one of those who made it out alive. About to suggest they mount and ride, he froze when the ground under them shook just enough to be felt, and immediately stopped.

"There will be more quakes," Winona predicted.

"On your horses, everyone," Nate directed. Another major tremor might tumble the high cliffs onto the valley floor. Or—he had a sudden, awful stab of fear—it might collapse the tunnel, severing the sole link to the outside world. Provided the tunnel had not already caved in.

At a gallop Nate led his family up the terraces. At the tree line he had no difficulty finding the trail his captors had used, and he moved along it at a reckless pace.

Winona rode double with Nevava. She was the only one with whom the boy was comfortable, and he clung to her as if she were his own mother. Patting his arm, she said, "You are safe now. No one will harm you." He did not respond.

No sounds broke the unnatural stillness. Nate rode with both hands on his Hawken, his wife's warning about the strange creatures fresh in his mind. But none appeared. Not a single animal stirred anywhere. The upheaval, he reflected, had cowed them into taking refuge in their dens and burrows.

At length Nate came to where the trail widened. In front of them reared the towering cliff. At its base was the dark rectangle that marked the entrance to the tunnel. Eagerly, Nate went to ride into it. Then he saw the opening clearly and an oath escaped his lips.

They were too late. The roof had buckled. A giant slab blocked the entrance, a slab so heavy it would take a hundred men to budge it.

Vaulting from the saddle, Nate conducted a closer inspection. He was elated to find a gap on the right side of the slab, a gap barely wide enough for a horse to squeeze through. Poking his head in, he tried to see how far back the gap extended, but it was pitch black. "We need torches," he announced.

With Zach's help, Nate constructed three. First they broke short limbs and trimmed them. Next they uprooted tall dry weeds, which they wound tight around one end of each limb, using whangs from Nate's hunting shirt to tie the weeds fast.

As he took out his fire steel and flint, Nate commented, "Maybe it would be better if I went in by my lonesome, just to make sure it's safe."

"We will stick together," Winona said. She would rather share his fate than be trapped in that horrible valley without him.

"What if another quake hits and the whole cliff comes crashing down?" Nate asked. If any of them had to die, he would gladly sacrifice himself to spare them.

"What will be, will be."

"We're with Ma on this one, Pa," Zach chimed in, and his sister nodded in agreement.

To try to talk them out of it would waste precious time. Every minute they squandered increased the likelihood of another severe earthquake erupting. Nate lit the torches, passing one to his wife and one to Zach.

Grasping the third, the mountain man entered the tunnel. He had to tug on the reins when the big black balked, and reluctantly it followed him. Three-fourths of the tunnel was gone, jumbled rubble all that remained. Some had spilled into the gap.

Nate stepped over a small boulder and advanced

briskly, holding the torch well in front. He did not like the feeling of being hemmed in, of having untold tons of solid rock and earth above and around him, ready to enfold him in its stony grip.

Winona gave the mare's reins to Zach, clasped her daughter's hand, and filed in. Nevava dogged their heels, following so closely that he bumped into her now and then. "Stay calm," she said in Ute. In English, she called back, "Can you handle those three by yourself, son?"

"I'll do just dandy, Ma," Zach replied. But the truth was that he could not lead his bay, the mare, and the pony in single file; their reins were not long enough. So he resorted to a rope, linking them by their necks. Pulling roughly, he hurried to catch up with his folks.

Nate King was beginning to think he had made a grave mistake. The gap had narrowed a couple of inches and the roof lowered a few, besides. What if there was no way through? How would he get the horses back out when they couldn't turn around?

Navigating the gloomy tunnel was like winding through the bowels of the earth. From time to time Nate heard dirt rattle down from above. More nerve-racking were the creaks and groans that testified to the tremendous pressure being exerted on the tunnel from all sides. It would not take much to bring the whole mess crashing down.

Around the next bend Nate beheld a ghastly spectacle. Some of the fleeing Anasazis had not made it out. Dozens had been partially buried, their smashed figures sprawled amid gore and blood. Shattered bones gleamed palely. Already the reek of death hung heavy. Bitter bile rose into Nate's mouth, and he spat it out.

Revulsion seized Evelyn. Averting her eyes, she dug her nails into her mother's palm and wished they were out in the open. If they ever made it home she was never going to leave again.

The passage of time became like the tunnel itself, dragging endlessly by. Nate's torch had about burned itself out when the stallion nickered loudly. The next moment the walls jiggled and the solid rock over his head sagged and split with hairline cracks. With nowhere to run, all Nate could do was fling an arm over his head.

The tremor lasted only a few moments. "Hurry," Winona urged after the trembling stopped. They had lived through that one, but they might not live through the next.

Nate did not need any encouragement. Soon his torch flickered its last and he flipped it onto the rubble. From then on he had to grope along in near-total darkness. Twice he stubbed a finger. Once he banged his shin.

There was no describing the delicious sensation that coursed through the trapper when a puff of wind caressed his face. It galvanized him into doubling his stride. He broke into a grin when at long, long last the tunnel ended and stars shone overhead. "We're out!" he exclaimed.

The air was wonderfully fresh, delightfully clean, unlike the air in the valley, which had been so thick and humid and tainted with a faint sweetish scent. As Nate turned to make sure his loved ones were safe, a bat flitted close above them.

Fleeting dizziness assailed him. For several bizarre seconds, Nate had the impression that the bat was ten times its normal size, and that its mouth was ringed with teeth as long as his Green River knife. Then the dizziness faded, the illusion vanished. Not knowing what to make of it, he shrugged and inhaled deeply, again and again.

Winona and the children were imitating him. "Where is the mist?" she asked. "And those red wolves?"

"Gone with the wind, like the Anasazis" was Nate's answer. "The same as we should be."

Off into the wilderness they trotted, into the wilderness they knew and loved, the wilderness they called home.

#45

WILDERNESS
IN CRUEL CLUTCHES

David Thompson

Zach King, son of legendary mountain man Nate King, is at home in the harshest terrain of the Rockies. But nothing can prepare him for the perils of civilization. Locked in a deadly game of cat-and-mouse with his sister's kidnapper, Zach wends his way through the streets of New Orleans like the seasoned hunter he is. Yet this is not the wild, and the trappings of society offer his prey only more places to hide. Dodging fists, knives, bullets and even jail, Zach will have to adjust to his new territory quickly—his sister's life depends on it.

PETER DAWSON

FORGOTTEN DESTINY

Over the decades, Peter Dawson has become well known for his classic style and action-packed stories. This volume collects in paperback for the first time three of his most popular novellas—all of which embody the dramatic struggles that made the American frontier unique and its people the stuff of legends. The title story finds Bill Duncan on the way to help his friend Tom Bostwick avoid foreclosure. But along the trail, Bill's shot, robbed and left for dead—with no memory of who he is or where he was going. Only Tom can help him, but a crooked sheriff plans to use Bill as a pawn to get the Bostwick spread for himself. Can Bill remember whose side he's supposed to be on before it's too late?

LOREN ZANE GREY

AMBUSH FOR LASSITER

Framed for a murder they didn't commit, Lassiter and his best pal Borling are looking at twenty-five years of hard time in the most notorious prison of the West. In a daring move, they make a break for freedom—only to be double-crossed at the last minute. Lassiter ends up in solitary confinement, but Borling takes a bullet to the back. When at last Lassiter makes it out, there's only one thing on his mind: vengeance.

RIDERS TO MOON ROCK

ANDREW J. FENADY

Like the stony peak of Moon Rock, Shannon knew what it was to be beaten by the elements yet stand tall and proud despite numerous storms. Shannon never quite fit in with the rest of the world. First raised by Kiowas and then taken in by a wealthy rancher, he found himself rejected by society time after time. Everything he ever wanted was always just out of his grasp, kept away by those who resented his upbringing and feared his ambition. But Shannon is determined to wait out his enemies and take what is rightfully his—no matter what the cost.

Dorchester Publishing Co., Inc.
P.O. Box 6640
_____5332-2
Wayne, PA 19087-8640
$5.99 US/$7.99 CAN

Please add $2.50 for shipping and handling for the first book and $.75 for each additional book. NY and PA residents, add appropriate sales tax. No cash, stamps, or CODs. Canadian orders require $2.00 for shipping and handling and must be paid in U.S. dollars. Prices and availability subject to change. **Payment must accompany all orders.**

Name: _____

Address: _____

City: _____ State: _____ Zip: _____

E-mail: _____

I have enclosed $_____ in payment for the checked book(s).

CHECK OUT OUR WEBSITE! www.dorchesterpub.com
_____ Please send me a free catalog.